The Curse of February Fourteenth

Christian Contemporary Romance

Three Rivers Ranch Romance™
Book 13

Liz Isaacson

Copyright © 2020 by Elana Johnson, writing as Liz Isaacson

All rights reserved.

No part of this book may be reproduced in any form or by any electronic or mechanical means, including information storage and retrieval systems, without written permission from the author, except for the use of brief quotations in a book review.

ISBN-13: 978-1-63876-343-7

"Lead me in thy truth, and teach me: for thou art the God of my salvation; on thee do I wait all the day."
∼*Psalms 25:5*

Chapter One

Cal Hodgkins dusted his palms together as he left the stables at Bowman's Breeds, located out at Three Rivers Ranch. He took a moment to enjoy the dusky light and perfect temperatures at this time of year. October was definitely the best month to be outside in Texas.

"You goin' to the dance tonight?" Garth Ahlstrom paused as he walked past, fully turning when Cal didn't answer right away. "There's dancing," the foreman of the ranch continued, a playful twinge in his tone. "Cookies. Costumes. Girls." A full-fledged smile galloped across his face with the last word.

Cal gave him an obligatory smile. He liked dancing, that was for sure. And cookies. He could do without the costumes, though he'd sent his six-year-old daughter a yellow princess dress so she could be appropriately dressed for her first grade Halloween party. Her mother and his ex-wife had sent pictures from the festivities earlier that day.

"Maybe," Cal said, thinking of his quiet cabin and the grilled cheese sandwich he could enjoy with a documentary about professional wrestling he'd found last weekend but hadn't had time to watch yet.

Garth, another silver-haired man like Cal, ducked his hat and continued on his way. Done with the horse care for the day, Cal strolled toward his cabin, his mind already wandering through the fields at the ranch he loved so much.

"You goin' to the dance?" Sawyer asked.

"Maybe," Cal told the cowhand.

Step, step, step.

"You goin' to the dance?" Beau asked.

"Maybe," Cal told his next-door neighbor.

He'd just reached his steps when Bennett stuck his head out of the barn doors. "A bunch of us are fixin' to go to the dance at seven-thirty." He grinned at Cal like they were old pals. Sure, Cal liked hanging out with the boys, but that was exactly the problem.

They were boys, none of them over thirty.

He was the only one who'd been married, the only one with a child who came to the ranch every other weekend, the only one who lived in a cowboy cabin alone.

"You're welcome to come." Bennett stepped out of the barn fully and leaned against the side of it.

The Curse of February Fourteenth

"I don't—"

"Come on," Bennett said. "You can't stay cooped up here all weekend. It's Halloween." He said it like Halloween was some great holiday, not to be missed.

Cal couldn't say he didn't fit with the other boys, wasn't interested in women, even though at thirty-nine-years-old he *didn't* fit and he *wasn't* interested in finding another mother for Sabrina.

But a companion for himself.... He sighed. "Seven-thirty?"

Bennett whooped and crossed the gravel path between the barns and the cabins. "You'll have fun, Cal."

"What are you dressing up as?"

"Cowboys." Bennett grinned and practically skipped back into the barn.

Cal couldn't help chuckling, and he had to admit that his heart took a bit of courage at not having to spend the evening alone. He usually liked being alone, but it had been a difficult week of work, dealing with a couple of pregnant horses on the ranch and then an accident at Brynn's that left two of her champion trainees hobbling around.

He hurried into his cabin and showered, putting on his best cowboy clothes, the ones he normally wore to church each Sunday. He got his grilled cheese and he managed to squeeze in a few minutes of that documentary before he headed through the barns to the parking lot. He didn't have to look far to find the boys heading into town.

The truck looked full already, with four men piled in the back. Their laughter rang through the clear air and almost made Cal turn around and go on home.

But Bennett had seen him, and he waved and said, "C'mon, Cal. We're gonna be late."

"It's seven-twenty-five," Cal said as he appraised the options for seating.

"Saved you a spot in the cab." Bennett grinned at him and leaned closer. "Had to convince Sawyer that the old man needed it." He laughed as he danced away from Cal's disdainful look. "Get in, Cal."

Cal got in. The forty-five minute drive into Three Rivers was filled with chatter between Bennett and his cabin mate, Beau. All the boys at the ranch called them B&B, because they never seemed to go anywhere without the other. As if their similarities weren't already enough, they were dating a set of sisters in town, who of course, would be at the dance tonight.

Cal listened to them talk about how they'd recognize the girls, as they were very excited about the prospect of a masked ball.

That got Cal's attention. "Masks?"

"All the women are wearing masks," Bennett said. "I just know I'm gonna fail at picking out Ruby."

"So I'm not even going to know who I'm dancing with?" Cal shifted on the seat.

"Nope."

Cal looked out the window, running through his

The Curse of February Fourteenth

options. He could go get ice cream at the shop down the street, wander the town until Bennett called and said it was time to go. He could—

"You're going," Bennett said. "I can practically see what you're thinkin'."

"What if I have to dance with Margaret?" Cal asked, not wanting to be rude, but, well, he simply couldn't do that again. Not that he'd ever danced with her, because the very idea sent a shudder through his muscles.

"Oh, Margaret," B&B said at the same time. They exchanged a glance, which didn't lift Cal's spirits at all.

"You guys gotta keep her away from me," Cal said.

"We've gotta—" Beau started at the same time Bennett said, "Sure, boss. Double wing men, at your service." He turned toward the downtown park, where the summer dances and other town festivals were always held. With three blocks still to go, the vehicles started thickening along the curbs.

Bennett pulled over into the next spot he saw and everyone piled out of the truck. Seven cowboys made quite the scene as they made their way to the party in full swing in the park. Cal automatically hung back while the other boys forged on, almost infected by the vibe in the country music staining the air.

Cal had fallen back three paces before Bennett turned to find him. "C'mon, boss," he called, and Cal wished he wouldn't call him "boss." He wasn't anyone's boss; it was just something Bennett called every man older than him.

Cal didn't come on. Something shook him inside. Probably all the bodies on the dance floor that had been laid over the grass. Or the dozens of people who wore masks. Any of them could be Margaret.

He lifted a red plastic cup of punch to his lips and drank the sugary-sweet liquid. Maybe he could just hang out here until he was sure Margaret wasn't here.

"C'mon." Bennett shouldered him, and Cal tried to twist away, only to find his second wingman there to block him. Together, B&B practically shoved him away from the refreshment tables.

"She's the one," Bennett said under his breath and pointed to a tall, lithe woman wearing a tight pair of black jeans, a tank top in the same shade, and a brilliant pair of orange monarch butterfly wings.

Her sun-kissed skin shone like the moon among all the black she wore—including a mask in the shape of butterfly's wings.

She definitely wasn't Margaret, and Cal found himself voluntarily walking toward her. He glanced right, expecting to see Bennett there to give him some advice, but Cal was very much on his own.

The butterfly wore a pair of black cowgirl boots with pale blue stitching in the shape of wings. She seemed hardly able to walk in the boots, but she continued toward him as if they were tethered together by some unknown line.

"Hey," Cal said when they were a few paces apart.

She didn't speak, but simply stared at him with blue-gray eyes behind the black mask.

A ballad came over the speakers. "You wanna dance?" Cal's voice seemed stuck in his throat, but sound managed to cross the space between them.

She nodded, and Cal extended his hand toward her. Her fingers were long, her skin tanned, her muscles defined. She stood only a few inches shorter than him, and she touched him with the grace and power of an athlete.

He wondered who she was, and when she'd come to town, as he'd never seen her before. And he liked to think he would've remembered. Of course, he didn't get to town much, other than church and the occasional grocery store run, but still. Talk of this woman would've made it through the cowboys in a matter of days.

Cal put one hand on her waist and she put one hand on his shoulders. They swayed, and Cal cursed himself for his slow tongue. But Butterfly didn't seem to have any problem with his lack of conversation, and she made no attempt to make small talk.

"Are you new in town?" he finally asked.

"Yes," she said. He could barely hear her, and he wanted to categorize the sound of her voice.

"What brings you to Three Rivers?"

"Not much." She lifted one sexy shoulder in a shrug.

Cal swallowed, wishing for that punch. He glanced around, trying to find a familiar face and being met with only blurred features and garish masks.

Butterfly stumbled in her too-big boots, and Cal steadied her. He tipped his head down, the brim of his hat nearly touching her forehead. Her wings bobbled, and a chuckle covered the awkwardness between them.

"You okay?" he asked.

"Just fine." She strengthened her grip on his shoulder, and he didn't mind that one little bit. "What's your name?" she asked.

"Cal Hodgkins."

A quick smile passed her lips but it didn't even get close to her eyes. He watched her, sensing something turbulent had brought her to Three Rivers. He understood the feeling, the pull the town had to wounded souls. He'd come to Three Rivers after his divorce four years ago, thinking he'd just stay for the night, thinking he was just passing through.

Then he'd met Heidi Ackerman in her bakery, and the woman had found out he was a veterinarian, and that was that. Cal didn't know that at the time, but he could see it now. Could see God's hand in leading Cal to that bakery, on that day, at that time. Heidi was Squire's mother, and Squire owned the ranch that had given Cal a purpose in his life. In many ways, that quick stop at the bakery for breakfast had saved Cal's life.

The song ended, and Butterfly stepped out of his arms. Cal's hands fell to his sides, lifeless. A sense of complete emptiness filled him, for no reason he could understand.

She ducked her head and a lock of dark hair fell across

her mask. She pushed it back and shot him the first smile he'd seen from her.

Her eye caught something over his shoulder and all happiness left her features. "I have to go," she said.

"Wait. What's your name?" Cal called after her, but the butterfly spun and hurried away. She stumbled, almost tripped, and continued. She reached the edge of the dance floor, the edge of the crowd. If she left the area, the darkness would swallow her in those dark clothes.

Cal hurried after her. "Wait," he tried again.

She glanced over her shoulder, and that was her undoing. She stepped onto the grass and down she went. Hard, too.

Cal shot forward, ready to help her up, help her back into his arms, where he wanted her to stay until he could get her name and phone number. But she was more agile than he'd given her credit for.

She leapt to her feet and took off into the darkness, leaving behind one black cowboy boot.

Cal reached the spot where she'd fallen, and he searched the darkness for a glimmer of her wings. "Wait," he said softly, to himself, before bending to pick up the winged cowgirl boot.

Chapter Two

Katrina couldn't believe she'd gone to this small-town party. She'd known it was a mistake, but her costume was a simple affair her roommate had on-hand as her "back-up costume." A pair of wings. A mask. A set of too-big cowgirl boots, both of which she really needed for her new job out at Bowman's Breeds the following week. Now she'd have to buy another pair.

"It's just money," she muttered to herself. If there was one thing Trina had, it was money. But she'd learned that money didn't buy happiness, or love, or privacy, something the Beatles had never sung about. And privacy was extremely important to Trina Salisbury.

But, oh, how that cowboy had called to her. Tall, and broad, with silver hair peeking out from underneath his black cowboy hat. She'd been drawn to him as if she were the south end of a magnet and he the north.

She ducked behind a thick tree trunk and reached down to remove the other boot. A sigh slipped through her lips. Libby would be so disappointed. She'd shopped for two hours for those boots. At least the wings and mask were still in place. Trina wished she could wear the mask all day, everyday. At least until the story of her breakup and subsequent disappearance got buried by something more interesting on the sports news channels.

An image of Carlos's face flashed through her mind, and Trina straightened. No one here knew about their messy, now broken relationship. It was why the Texas panhandle was perfect for someone like her. The people here liked cowboys, and horses, and football. Tennis wasn't anywhere near their radar, and no one had recognized her in the three days since she'd arrived in town.

Her appointment at the salon the following day would further ensure she remained a nameless, unremarkable addition to this town.

Please help me blend in here, she thought, wondering where the mental energy went. No matter where, she managed to slip under the cover of darkness and back to her apartment around the corner from the bank without running into anyone else.

Libby didn't return home for hours, by which time Trina had carefully hung the monarch wings and changed out of her tight black clothing. She pretended to be asleep, even when her giggly, auburn-haired roommate whispered, "Trina? Are you really asleep?"

The Curse of February Fourteenth

No, she wasn't really asleep. She'd slept little since the public break-up, her nerves always on standby, her mind always revolving around whether the cashier at the gas station in a town she didn't even know the name of might be looking at her curiously.

She woke the following morning, so she knew she'd fallen asleep at some point. But she didn't feel refreshed or ready to face the day. It had been a long time since she didn't know exactly what every minute of every day would look like, smell like, feel like. A long time since she'd had this level of white-hot anxiety running through her, and it wasn't because she was up against the number one player in the world.

No, this sick feeling in her stomach—this sick feeling that never went away—was because she was trying to be something she wasn't. And she'd never done that before. When she was ranked number nineteen in the world, she played like it. She trained and fought and ran down every ball until she was in the top ten women in the world.

And then she played like them. All the way to number one—where she wanted to end her career.

But Carlos—

"Hey, you're up." Libby beamed at her as she secured her hair into a ponytail. "I'm going hiking with this dreamy man I met last night. You want to come?"

"No," Trina said automatically. No way she was getting in between Libby and this dreamy guy.

"Did you even stay for one dance last night?" Libby sat on her bed opposite of Trina.

"Yes." A smile ghosted across her face at the mere thought of Cal Hodgkins. "One dance."

Libby shook her head, a low giggle coming out of her throat. "I guess that's what you promised."

"I texted you when I got home too," she said.

Libby patted her knee like this big bad Texan world would eat Trina right up if it weren't for her. "Yes, you did. Thank you for that." She bounced to her feet. "Well, I don't want to keep Levi waiting!" She grabbed her purse and slipped on some very not-hiking shoes before turning back. "You'll have to tell me all about your 'one dance' when I get back."

"Sure, yeah," Trina agreed just to get Libby to go. It was exactly that kind of conversation that had Trina faking sleep and wondering when Libby would return so Trina could make sure she wasn't there.

Libby waved and skipped out the front door, leaving Trina with her misery and a gush of guilt flowing through her. She shouldn't be so annoyed that Libby wanted to talk. She'd given Trina the room sight-unseen. The fact that Trina had said, "I'll pay for six months up front," had probably helped.

Apologize later, she told herself as she went to get ready for her hair appointment.

* * *

The Curse of February Fourteenth

Monday morning found her in a new pair of cowgirl boots. This time, brown leather peeked up at her from beneath the hem of her jeans, but they didn't make her a cowgirl. But they made her look like one, and that was all she needed until she could figure out how to actually become one.

"I'm looking for Brynn?" she said upon arriving out at Three Rivers Ranch and entering the building she'd been told to look for.

A cowboy glanced over at her from a stack of shelves where he was working. "She's out in the stables."

"Oh, um." Trina would need to look up exactly what a stable was, and she wondered for a flash of time if her phone had WiFi out here. She had a sinking feeling she'd need to learn a lot of horse vocabulary before the day ended.

"Cal will take you out." He nodded to someone behind Trina.

She spun, her heart—which had withered but not stopped beating these past few months—jumping to the back of her throat like a silly frog.

And there he stood. Easily the most handsome man Trina had ever laid eyes on—and she'd traveled around the world since she was ten years old—Cal stood a few inches taller than her, wearing that delicious black hat and a smile that slipped the longer she stared at him.

Self-consciously, she reached up and tucked her now-short hair behind her ear. It didn't stay but flopped right back out of place. She'd bleached and dyed her hair the color of butterscotch, and then cut ten inches off it so it now stuck out of her head at odd angles. At least to her. She was used to pulling it into a ponytail and going, but that morning, she'd had to primp and prod and flat-iron the short pieces into their proper places.

"Mornin'," Cal said, his voice somewhere on the awed scale. Probably close to a seven or eight.

Trina couldn't respond. Cal blinked at her before glancing to the other cowboy. "Who is she?"

"She didn't say."

"Trina," she blurted, finally able to get her name out. It was safe; she hadn't told him at the dance a couple of nights ago. "I'm Trina Salisbury, and Brynn hired me for some, um, general horse care." She did a little curtsy without knowing why. "It's my first day."

"She's in the stables," the cowboy said again, sliding a file into a slot in the bookcase.

Cal ran his eyes down the length of her body and back to the hat that felt silly perched on her head. "All right, then. Come with me." He maneuvered past her into the narrow hallway that led to a door with sunlight streaming through it.

"You haven't been here before?" he asked as he stepped through the door and held it open for her.

"No." The smell of hay and rot and animal dung met her nose, and she suddenly regretted her snap decision to work on a farm. A ranch. The sign had definitely said Three Rivers *Ranch*.

"She hired me over the phone." Trina glanced at Cal, thinking he'd soothe the bats flapping through her insides. But his handsomeness only stirred the mammals into a riot.

He nodded, pressed his hat further onto his head, and started along a fence that separated the humans from the horses.

And oh, my, there were a lot of horses. Trina's hand fluttered to her throat, sure she was about to throw up. What had she been thinking? She'd been hitting tennis balls for twenty-four years, not hauling hay or saddling horses. She didn't even know how to haul hay or saddle horses. And she didn't think there would be a handy manual tacked to the wall to help her out.

"What do you do here?" she asked Cal, trying to get her heartbeat to even out. *It'll be fine, she told herself. Brynn said this job was moving horses from one place to the other. Giving baths. Stuff like that.*

"Stuff like that," had been Brynn's exact words, and now Trina wondered what "stuff" she really meant.

Honestly, anything would be better than being caged inside a giant mansion in the hills above LA, watching the paparazzi as they jostled for position right up against her gate.

"I'm a veterinary technician," Cal said over his shoulder. "Squire Ackerman—he owns the ranch—is the lead vet. But I have a specialization in large animal care, and with all the horses out here, Squire needed a Number Two."

Cal was anything but Number Two, but Trina kept that thought to herself. Still, she enjoyed the view from the back as he led her out to a large, square-U shaped building with a wide aisle down the middle.

Horse stalls lined both sides, and every item was hung exactly in its place. Cal moved with easy strides like he'd worn cowboy boots his whole life.

Trina's feet slipped and her toes pinched inside the unyielding leather boots. He turned the corner to reveal even more stalls, and Trina's breath caught in her throat. There were way more horses here than she'd ever imagined.

"There she is," Cal said, nodding with his head in a very cowboy way. His Texas drawl shot shivers right down Trina's legs, and she followed his gaze as she drew in a shaky breath.

A woman wearing jeans, a long-sleeved purple shirt, and a cowgirl hat stood at a stall, stroking an impossibly huge black horse. Her blonde braid hung down her back, and she looked every bit as country-western as Cal.

Trina had never felt so out of place.

"Thanks," she managed to say before she walked away.

"Hey," Cal said in a gentle voice. Trina turned back to him. He once again devoured her with his eyes, and

The Curse of February Fourteenth

Trina's face flushed with heat. "Do I know you? Have we met?"

Her lungs seized, forgetting how to breathe in her most crucial moments. "I—I don't think so. I've only just come to town for the job."

Cal stalked closer, his gorgeous lake-blue eyes narrowing. "You've only just come to town?"

"Well, I've been here for a couple of weeks." She almost cringed with the lie. A fib, really. And who cared?

Cal would care, she thought. Though she hardly knew him, he seemed like the type to value honesty and integrity above all else.

Which was exactly why he could never know who she really was, where she really came from, or why she'd come to Three Rivers. He certainly wouldn't be interested in getting to know her then, though he wore the look of a starved man staring at Thanksgiving dinner right now.

"Thanks," she said with a little wave before turning and hurrying toward Brynn. She felt split down the middle—half of her really wanted to see Cal again, and the other half hoped they never had cause to bump into one another out here at the ranch.

Chapter Three

Cal watched the tall, lithe woman with neat muscles in her arms and legs walk away from him. She reminded him of the butterfly.

He shook his head.

That woman had possessed long, dark hair the color of Kit Kat's tail. He shook his head harder. "Shouldn't compare a pretty woman to a horse," he muttered to himself.

Butterfly had also had blue-gray eyes harboring storms, but Trina's eyes were all blue, with only a tremor of fear in them. Fear that was completely reasonable on her first day of a new job.

Cal turned away from her, the cowgirl boot he'd taken back to his cabin and thoughtfully placed on his mantel mocking him. He'd asked the other boys who'd gone to the dance if they knew who she was. Looked for the woman at church. He'd even put a bug in Heidi's ear about anyone new who had come to town.

No one had been able to help him learn anything new about his mysterious butterfly.

He stopped by Kit Kat's stall just to see the old bay horse. He didn't work ranches or rodeo circuits anymore, but Kit Kat was a loyal friend who always seemed eager to say hello to Cal when he stopped by.

"Hey there, fella." Cal stroked the horse's cheeks. "You haven't seen a beautiful woman wearing wings, have you?"

The horse actually nickered, and Cal grinned at him. "That's what I thought." He sighed as he headed back into the front office to pick up the list of horses that needed attention today. Of course he had the two who'd been injured—Grand Junction and Honeybee—but Brynn also kept him on a pretty tight rotation with her other horses.

She did pay a third of his salary, so Cal didn't mind. He liked working with the horses at Courage Reins the best, as they were trained therapy equines, without temperaments or issues. Brynn's horses were told all day long how awesome they were, and some of them pranced around like they knew it.

Cal chuckled to himself that he was thinking about horses as people again. As he reached the door of the stable, he cast a long look over his shoulder, trying to conjure up the sound of Butterfly's voice to see if it matched Trina's.

The Curse of February Fourteenth

He couldn't remember, and he turned away from the stable—and all thoughts of the mysterious woman who had completely invaded his mind.

Cal put his energy to work, and enjoyed the cooler fall temperatures, his horses, and the steady beating of his heart. In his younger days, when he ran the rodeo circuit, he'd learned to listen to the pulse of his heart in his ears, feel it in his chest, before the run started.

He'd learned to trust himself by listening to his heartbeat. Learned to trust the pulses of the horses in his care. Learned to trust his instincts based on what the beats told him.

He caught sight of Trina as he left the stables in favor of lunch. She looked frazzled and kept running her hand over her hair like she couldn't understand what was going on. She danced away from the horse when she should've gone toward it, and Cal's lips twitched upward.

Brynn corrected her, and Cal started to duck his head just as Trina looked at him. A spark started in his gut, and he actually took a step toward her. She broke the connection between them as she took the reins from Brynn and started to lead the horse through a gate.

Foolishness filled Cal from bottom to top. What was wrong with him? Perhaps he hadn't dated in so long that every woman seemed wonderful.

That's not true, he told himself as he hurried out of the stable and toward the dirt road that would take him home. *You don't like Margaret.*

His phone rang as he mounted the steps to his cabin. Petra. His mouth turned dry as he swiped on the call. "Petra?" he asked. "What's wrong? Is Sabrina okay?"

"Sabrina's fine," his ex-wife drawled. "Why do you always ask if she's okay?"

"I don't know," Cal said, avoiding the argument. He asked, because Petra only called when something wasn't okay. Otherwise, she texted.

He moved into the kitchen while Petra said, "We're catering a wedding next weekend, and I was wondering if you could take Sabrina even though it's not your turn."

"Of course." Cal pulled out a loaf of bread. "So I'll have her this weekend and next."

"Right."

"Maybe she could just stay with me on the ranch," he said. He didn't mind the hour-long drive to Pampa, where Petra lived with her mother and helped with the family restaurant that had been named a historical marker last year. "She'd have to miss school, but its just first grade. How much can they be doing?"

"They do a lot," Petra said, a touch of defensiveness in her voice.

"I'll read with her every night," Cal said. He wasn't sure why he wanted his daughter to come, only that he never got to see her during the week because of school, and he missed her.

"They do math too," Petra said.

The Curse of February Fourteenth

"I can do math." Cal spread peanut butter on his bread and opened the fridge to find the strawberry rhubarb jam Miss Kelly had made earlier that fall. His jar was empty.

"I'll talk to Sabrina."

"Have her call me after school," Cal said, unwilling to let Petra have that much control over the conversation with their six-year-old.

"All right," she said moments before saying good-bye and ending the call.

Cal ate his lonely lunch at the kitchen table that only had two chairs. He wasn't sure what a six-year-old would do all day while he worked with horses, but he had a television and a phone, and Sabrina had always enjoyed coming to the ranch.

He stood and washed his hands, unsatisfied from his meal of bread and peanut butter. But this afternoon, he was working over at Courage Reins, and that lifted his spirits. Reese always had candy at the front desk, which he manned, and sometimes Pete brought in lunch for everyone.

Oh, yes, Cal's first stop would be the conference room to see if he could fill his stomach with something better.

He moved toward the front door and had his hand on the knob when his gaze landed on the black cowgirl boot resting on his mantel. The light blue stitching flamed up, reminding him of those beautiful wings, the tight, black clothing Butterfly had worn, the haunted quality in her eyes that had called to Cal's soul.

He reached out and traced on fingertip along the upper part of the stitching. *Who was she?* he wondered. Had she left town already?

Help me find her, he prayed, quite sure that God didn't concern himself with desperate cowboys in the Texas Panhandle but determined to keep praying just in case He did.

PETE HAD BROUGHT in doughnuts that morning, and several remained in the long brown box on the conference room table. Cal helped himself before stopping by the front desk to chat with Reese for a few minutes.

The other cowboy handed him a list of three horses Pete had identified for check-ups that day, and Cal took the hint to get to work.

Courage Reins shared barn and stable space with the ranch, so Cal headed across the street to find the appointed horses. The ranch didn't have quite the five-star accommodations as Brynn did, so he had to open a door to enter the stable.

And a horse pushed its way right out, nosing him in the chest and causing Cal to stumble backward.

"Whoa," he said, noticing the wild look in the horse's

eyes. "Whoa there." He caught hold of the reins and managed to get the horse stilled.

"Oh, you got him." Trina came running down the aisle, panic in her expression that matched Cash the Check's.

"This is a champion barrel racing horse," Cal said. "What are you doin' with him over here?" He reached up and stroked the horse's neck, pulling the reins tighter to communicate to the animal that he was okay. Safe. Someone else was in control here, and he could just relax.

"Brynn told me to bring him over here because he's...." She cleared her throat and shuffled her feet around like the cement beneath her boots was made of lava.

"He's a stud," Cal said, heat rising to his own face for some reason.

"Right. A stud." Trina exhaled. "And he sort of got all, I don't know, freaked out or something, and I lost my grip on him."

Cal liked the sound of her voice, the way she spoke with a calm lilt to her words. She definitely wasn't from Texas, but he didn't know where she came from.

"So who's he supposed to be with?"

"Iron Beauty."

Cal clucked his tongue as he started walking and Cash the Check lowered his head and plodded along beside him. "Iron Beauty is in the next stable over. Come on, I'll take you."

"Thanks." Trina caught up to him and matched her stride to his. "This is a big place, and it's—"

"Your first day," Cal said at the same time she did. He grinned down at her. "Did you get lunch?"

"Sort of."

"Sort of?"

"I ate a handful of crackers on the way over here."

"That's not lunch."

She lifted one shoulder in a shrug Cal could only classify as sexy. He tried to think of something intelligent to say. "You gotta take a lunch out here. There will always be something keeping you from eating. But it's not healthy to work straight through."

She glanced up at him, a shy smile staining her face. It reached her eyes, lighting them up, and Cal felt like he'd been kicked in the chest by a champion bronc riding horse. One that could buck hard. "You sound like you've had some experience with skipping lunch."

"More than I want to admit." He chuckled as he reached the door to the correct stable. He paused, wanting to draw out their encounter.

"So no skipping lunch," she said, reciting it like she was making a list of things to improve upon for Day Two of her new job.

"Nope."

"Anything else I should know?"

Cal was sure there were dozens of things he could tell her that would make her life easier out here at the ranch.

The Curse of February Fourteenth

"You've got a hat," he said, letting himself scan her body again. He'd done it a couple of times that morning, and she was just as curvy and beautiful now as she had been then.

All his subdued thoughts surged forward, making his next tip one word.

"Sunscreen."

"I'm used to being outside all day," she said.

"Water?" Why it sounded like a question he wasn't sure.

"I *am* thirsty."

"Well, let's get this stud delivered to his lady, and then we'll head over to my cabin and get you a drink." Cal couldn't let a woman go thirsty on the ranch. That wouldn't be gentlemanly.

He found Garth waiting outside Iron Beauty's stall, and he delivered Cash the Check to the foreman with a tip of his hat.

It almost felt natural to reach for Trina's hand and lead her down the gravel path to his cabin. He stuffed his hands in his pockets instead.

"You'll probably want to wear long sleeves or a jacket once winter comes," he said, noticing her tanned arms.

"Does it get very cold here?"

"Where are you from?"

"California."

"Colder than California," he said as he went up the steps to his cabin. He opened the door and let her enter first. He went into the kitchen to get some ice water, letting her examine his place.

"What's this?" she asked, and Cal swung his attention from the ice cube tray to find her holding the black cowgirl boot.

He spasmed, sending ice cubes all over the floor. His phone rang at that moment, and he hid his flaming face as he turned to answer his daughter's call.

Chapter Four

"Hey, baby," Cal drawled from the kitchen. Trina's stomach flipped over once, then twice. She looked down at her cowgirl boot and back to the very prominent spot where he'd placed it.

Why she'd brought it up, she didn't know. Fishing for compliments?

You should tell him that boot is yours. She set it back down on the mantel like it had spontaneously burst into flames. *It obviously means something to him.*

"We'll have so much fun this weekend," he said, and Trina's doubts roared to life. Just because he had the boot above his fireplace didn't mean anything. And she didn't want him to know they'd met at the masked ball. Number one, he'd ask a lot of questions about the change to her hair.

But he knew her name now, and where she was from, and panic bolted through her so powerfully, her legs shook. He couldn't know who she was. Which meant he couldn't know they'd met before.

Trina had left her tennis self behind. Gone was the dark hair. Gone was the ultra-confidence that drew rich and powerful men to her.

Though, one glance at where Cal still stood in the kitchen, and she felt a rich and powerful attraction to him.

"Listen, sweetheart, I have to go. I'll see you Friday night." He grinned at whatever the person on the other end of the line said, and ended with, "Love you too, baby. 'Bye."

So he had a girlfriend. Great.

Trina had never needed a drink so badly, but she'd wanted to escape one other situation more than this one, so she stayed put, right there in the man's living room.

He finished filling her glass and presented her with an ice cold drink, his gaze sweeping over the cowgirl boot and landing on her.

"Where are you living?" he asked.

"Just around the corner from the bank," she said. "I have a roommate." She gulped the water to get herself to stop talking.

"Is she new in town too?"

"Who?"

"Your roommate."

"Oh, no. I think she's lived here for a while." Just the

state of Libby's bedroom testified of that. Trina was pretty sure Libby had mentioned having a cat, but Trina had never seen one in the apartment.

"Hmm."

"Why?"

His boots scuffed the floor as he shimmied around. He cleared his throat and Trina found a gorgeous blush staining his neck. She wanted to reach up and remove that cowboy hat, really see the full effect of his silver hair.

She reined in her scattering hormones, reminding herself that he was probably way too old for her.

"I'm looking for someone," he finally said. "Did you happen to go to the Halloween dance a few nights ago?"

The water sloshed in her stomach, reminding her that she'd eaten very little that day. She blinked, and the handsome features of Cal's face blurred. "No," she heard herself say. "But I think my roommate did."

Eagerness edged his eyes now. "Really?"

Trina needed to get out of there. Get out of there fast. "I better get back to Brynn," she said. She put the glass of water down directly next to the boot and yanked open the door.

The fresh air outside did nothing to curb the rising panic, and Trina knew she wouldn't be able to stop it. She flew down the stairs and around the side of Cal's cabin only moments before the anxiety peaked and the attack started.

Sweat formed all over her face and arms, leaving her

feeling clammy and cold though the winters Cal had mentioned certainly hadn't arrived yet.

Her breath came in quick pants no matter how she tried to draw in a deep lungful of oxygen. She bent over and braced her hands against her knees and let the waves of anxiety roll across her shoulders.

The panic ebbed as fast as it had risen, leaving Trina weak and exposed. She straightened, finally getting that deep breath she needed, and swung her attention away from the ranch and toward the wilds of the prairie.

She walked the length of Cal's house and stood at the corner of it, the waving grasses beyond his back fence a welcome balm to the busy morning she'd had.

Brynn could tell Trina was inexperienced, but she hadn't questioned her. Hadn't reprimanded her. Only worked with her with an extreme amount of patience. Trina was used to high-pressure situations—she actually thrived on them—so leading a horse hadn't been too bad.

The panic attacks were new though, and she still didn't have a handle on them. They always revolved around someone discovering who she was, and she'd left three other small towns like this one before arriving in Three Rivers.

She leaned against the wood of Cal's cabin, something whispering through her that she didn't want to leave this place. The longer she gazed at the beautiful horizon here, the more it calmed her.

"You okay?" Cal's voice behind her made her turn.

She wiped her forehead and noticed that he held her hat in his hands. "I'm okay, yeah."

He gestured with the hat back toward the front corner of the house. "I couldn't help but—" He swallowed hard. "Overhear. You seemed upset."

She glanced past him to where she'd stood. A window sat directly above that. Of course he'd overheard. Probably witnessed the whole thing. The fight left her body. Would it be so terrible if one man in one tiny Texas town knew who she was?

Yes, a voice shouted in her head.

That voice always won. That voice had led her to victory more times than Trina could count. That voice had helped her see reason when Carlos was caught cheating again. That voice had gotten her out of the very bad situation she'd found herself in.

That voice had brought her to Three Rivers.

"I have some anxiety," she said, matching her gaze to his, almost daring him to pity her or even so much as say anything. "That was an attack. I'm still learning how to work through them."

A frown marred his perfectly symmetrical features, pulling his left eyebrow down more than his right. "I'm sorry, Trina."

That was all. No advice. No more questions. Just sympathy. She peered at him and found him to be genuine, no ulterior motives.

He was utterly refreshing.

"My ex-wife suffers from some anxiety," he said, that frown still in place. "It's a tough thing I wouldn't wish on anyone." He extended her hat toward her, and she took a couple of steps to take it from him.

"Thank you," she murmured. After putting the hat back on, she faced the open land again. Cal joined her, only a foot away. It felt like leagues, especially when he tucked his hands into his pockets.

"So you're divorced?" she asked, her tone a forced casual he'd surely be able to hear.

"Yep. Four years now."

"Who's your girlfriend?"

"Girlfriend?"

"The woman you were talking to on the phone." Trina stole a glance at him and found him staring at her, wide-eyed, those electric blue eyes sinking right through her skin and into her bloodstream. Did he know how handsome he was? Could he even comprehend what he was doing to her pulse right now?

He tipped his head back and laughed, as if that would somehow decrease his attractiveness. It didn't. In fact, it made him even more desirable, because his laugh was a booming one that filled the sky and radiated pure joy.

"That wasn't my girlfriend," he said, still chuckling. He sobered and looked right at Trina, hooked her with those sharp eyes. "That was my daughter."

"Oh," left Trina's mouth. "How old is she?"

"Six."

Trina took the time to scan him from boots to hat. "You don't look old enough to have a six-year-old daughter."

"Really? You don't think all this silver hair qualifies me to have a six-year-old?"

She giggled, beyond glad when he swept off his cowboy hat to reveal a full head of that delightful hair.

"How old are you?" she asked.

He gave her a sideways look, the corners of his mouth pulling up. "If I tell you, will you tell me?"

"Sure."

"Most Southern women find it rude if a man asks their age."

She leaned into the cabin again, this flirting easier than anything she'd done since leaving California. "Well, I'm not a Southern woman."

He swallowed again, and when he looked at her, he wore a hunger in his eyes she didn't understand. "Thirty-nine."

Relief poured through her. He wasn't that much older than her, despite the silver hair. "Thirty-three."

He smiled to the waving grasses and turned back to the ranch. "Come on, I'll walk you back to Brynn's."

"You don't need to do that."

"I know." He went with her anyway, and Trina was glad to have the company, even if he stayed silent. He felt steady next to her. Strong. Calm. The exact opposite of how Trina had felt since leaving tennis, leaving California, leaving Carlos, leaving her whole life.

When they reached Brynn's, he touched the brim of his hat and turned to go back the way he'd come. He turned around and walked backward, calling, "Lunch at my place tomorrow?"

"Sure," she said before she could think.

He grinned, lifted one hand in a wave, and turned back around. Trina watched him go, unsure about what she'd just agreed to.

A date?

Just a friendly lunch in his cabin?

She groaned. How was she supposed to go back in there with that boot staring her in the face?

"Ah, there you are," Brynn said, poking her head out of the door. "Did you get Cash the Check over to his appointment?"

Trina nodded as she started to follow Brynn into the front office.

"Great. I've got a horse for you to exercise before you go."

"Yeah, okay," Trina said, wondering why a horse needed to exercise. Another thing to add to her growing list of *Things to Google When I Get Home.*

* * *

"So you really don't go to church?"

Trina rolled over and looked at Libby all dressed up in a black and red-flowered dress. Considering Trina was still in bed, unshowered, without a dress to her name—unless her tennis skirts counted—no, she really didn't go to church.

"You go on without me," she said.

"But I went without you last week." Libby pouted and the teenager act would've been complete with a little stamp of her heeled foot.

Trina pushed herself into a sitting position. "Look, Libby, I don't really go to church."

"But it's the best place to meet men."

Trina gave her roommate a patient smile while silently contradicting her. The ranch was definitely the best place to meet men. There were at least ten of them out there, single, and working with her in close quarters for hours everyday.

She didn't find any of them as intriguing as Cal, and she'd managed to eat lunch at his cabin a few times without completely falling apart. He didn't ask her about her roommate again, or the dance. Didn't even so much as glance toward the boot when they were together.

"I don't want to meet a man," Trina said, speaking the truth. Cal was different. Cal was...Cal. She wondered if he'd be at church with his daughter, thinking maybe it would be a good idea to see if Libby had anything Trina could borrow....

She then wondered how many churches there could possibly be in Three Rivers. Probably a dozen, and it would be impossible to know if Libby went to the same one Cal did. Then her pampering and borrowing would be for naught.

"Well, you'll at least come to the church dinner this weekend, right?"

"Church dinner?"

"The pastor puts on a Thanksgiving Day dinner for everyone. He provides all the turkey, and we bring the sides. It's a lot of food and fun...." Libby let her words hang there like turkey and mashed potatoes alone would be enough to entice Trina to come.

And because Trina had spent years eating bars specially formulated with exactly the right proportions of carbs and protein, she said, "Yeah, that sounds fun."

Libby squealed, pivoted on her heel, and left Trina to go back to sleep. She didn't, but began plotting ways she could work the church Thanksgiving Day dinner into her conversations with Cal. Maybe she could sleuth out whether he went to church and if so, which one.

She'd enjoyed talking to him this week, and she'd even managed to figure out a few things regarding the job. She could lead a horse now, feed and water the horses, shovel out stalls, and find her way around the ranch, Courage Reins, and Brynn's training facilities.

But if she were ever asked to ride a horse.... Well, that wouldn't go well. She couldn't even saddle one of the beasts, though she had been watching how-to videos online for the past few days. She'd found a really great channel and had been devouring the videos, from brushing down a horse to shoeing a horse.

Trina found she enjoyed the work. It was different than getting up at the crack of dawn to hit balls with Carlos. Different than going to the gym after eight hours on the courts and running until she felt like puking. Different than signing autographs, and flying all over the world, and always always always having to look perfect, act perfect, be perfect.

Her phone chimed, and she picked it up from the nightstand next to her bed. Her mom.

How did the new job go last week?

Great, Trina tapped out.

I'm glad. Still not going to tell me what it is?

I'm doing great, Mom. Really.

Your dad and I are worried about you. Jackie too.

Trina scoffed at the mention of her sister. Jackie had been texting since Trina left months ago. But it was never in the vein of worry or caring about where Trina was or how she was doing. Instead, she always mentioned Carlos and how upset he was that Trina had left him right in the middle of the tour.

As if Trina didn't know when she'd left. As if Carlos had a right to be upset after what he'd done.

I'm somewhere safe, and I have a job, and things are going really great. Trina sent the text, aware that she'd used *great* multiple times. She didn't know how else to help her mom. Even if things weren't going so well, even when she'd left Tempe in the middle of the night because she thought someone had recognized her at the grocery store, she'd still tell her mom things were great.

She simply wouldn't give her mother any more reasons to worry, and if that meant a little fib, then Trina was fine with that.

But she wasn't fibbing this time. For the first time since she'd left Carlos, left tennis, and left California, she really was doing pretty great.

She didn't need the money the job out at Bowman's Breeds provided, but she needed something to fill her time. Not one to be idle, Trina craved long hours filled with hard work that required the use of her muscles. And the ranch was a perfect place for that.

After realizing she wasn't going to fall back asleep, Trina got up and went into the kitchen of the tiny apartment she shared with Libby. The fridge didn't provide many options, but she managed to cobble together the ingredients to make a really good hamburger.

When Libby walked in an hour later, fresh from church, Trina had a burger for each of them with a sliver of cheese melted on, a special sauce she'd made by mixing ketchup and mayo, and a slice of tomato.

"You can cook?" Libby gazed at the food like it was manna from heaven.

"A little," Trina said. "Burgers." She nudged one of the

plates closer to Libby, who picked up the burger and took a bite.

"This is so good," she said with her mouth full.

Trina smiled. "It's my favorite food." She picked up her hamburger and bit into it, the *great*ness of her life at the moment out of this world.

Chapter Five

"Hey, you wanna go riding?" Cal swung his daughter's hand as they left church together.

"Can I ride Kit Kat?"

He beamed down at her carefree face. "Sure can." A rush of love for the towheaded girl filled him. "And I think I even have some real kit kats in my fridge."

"The fridge?" Sabrina wrinkled her nose the way she always did when she was confused. "Why do you put candy bars in the fridge?"

He chuckled. "It was an old trick I learned from my mom." Just the thought of his parents made him sigh. They still lived in Dallas, in the same suburban home where he'd grown up with a brother and two sisters.

"She used to put treats in the fridge she didn't want any of us kids to find." He opened the door to his truck and lifted Sabrina onto the seat, which elicited a giggle from her. "See, we weren't allowed to just open the fridge and get out whatever we wanted. So Momma put all her best stuff in there. Uncle Kyle was always tryin' to take my stuff, so I learned to put it in the fridge too."

"Uncle Kyle!" Sabrina said, her blue eyes brightening. "Does he still have that dog?"

It had been a while since Cal had taken Sabrina to see any of his siblings. His job at Three Rivers was seven-days-a-week demanding, and he only saw his daughter on weekends.

"He's havin' Thanksgiving dinner at his house in Austin this year," Cal said. "We should go find out."

"His dog was funny."

"He taught him those tricks, you know." Cal nodded toward her seat belt. "Buckle up." He went around the front of the truck, scanning the patrons still streaming from the church building. He'd managed to learn from Brynn that Trina's roommate was Libby Larsen, and while Cal wasn't super thrilled to talk to the clingiest woman in town, he did want to ask Libby if she'd seen the monarch butterfly at the masked ball.

He'd seen Libby at church previously, but she didn't seem to be there this week. His heart bobbed around in his chest, not fully anchored the way it should be. He wasn't sure why he cared about the butterfly so much.

Trina had been eating lunch with him when their schedules aligned, and he enjoyed her company. Once or twice, he'd even wondered if she could be the butterfly.

The Curse of February Fourteenth

She had similar features—the shape of her face, though most of it had been covered by the mask, the length of her limbs, and the way she held onto her vowels longer than most Texans.

Of course, she wasn't Texan, so that made sense.

Cal was just turning to get in the truck and take Sabrina horseback riding when he saw a flash of auburn hair.

"Bingo," he muttered to himself, yanking open the door. "I have to go talk to someone," he told his daughter. He stuck the key in the ignition and turned on the truck. "Heat it up for us, okay, baby?"

He closed the door without waiting for her to confirm. Libby was trailing two cowboys—Bennett and Sawyer, and Cal almost went right back to his truck. He'd already asked them both about the monarch butterfly, and he didn't want them to think he was still hung up on her.

But Cal was still hung up on her.

And so he renewed the purpose in his stride and called, "Libby?" while she was still several paces behind the other boys.

She turned toward him, and he lifted his hand in hello so she'd know he was the one who'd called. Her face scrunched up for a quick beat and then she smoothed over the confusion with an astronomical smile. "Cal Hodgkins." She swayed her hips as she stepped off the curb and joined him in the parking lot.

"Hey," he said, a bit breathless. "Listen, Trina said you went to the Halloween dance?"

"Yeah, but—"

Cal spoke over her, anxious to get this conversation done. "Did you see a woman there dressed like a monarch butterfly?" He watched her reaction carefully.

She blinked at him once, twice, three times. "I—don't know."

Exasperation bled through him. "She was wearing all black. Dark hair, bright orange wings." If Libby hadn't seen her, Cal couldn't be sure the butterfly even existed. Libby Larsen knew everyone in town, everything they did, even what kind of car they drove.

"Maybe," Libby said, growing more confused by the moment. "Why?"

"I...." Cal reconsidered his tactics. If he told her, it was possible the whole town would know by dinnertime. But if that meant he could find the butterfly.... "I danced with her," he said. "And I didn't get her name or number. I'm trying to find out who she was."

A light entered Libby's eyes. "Ooh, a mystery girl."

Cal groaned inwardly. "I suppose. Did you see her?"

"Yes, I saw her," Libby said.

Relief made Cal exhale his breath into a chuckle. "Do you know who she is?"

Libby looked over her shoulder to see if there was anyone lingering too close. Most of the patrons had already gone, and the near-winter wind whipped the early leaves that had fallen along the cement.

"I can find out," she said in a conspiring whisper. "Why don't you give me your number, and I'll call you when I find her." She held out her phone, a glint in her eyes Cal wasn't sure about.

He stared at the phone, indecision raging within him. In the end, he wanted to know who the butterfly was, and if the toll was his number in Libby Larsen's phone, he'd pay it.

"So you'll listen to Trina and do whatever she says," Brynn told Sabrina the following morning. "She's going to be feeding the outside herd today, so you can tag along with her."

Cal smiled down at his daughter, then flashed a grateful look in Brynn's direction before settling his gaze on Trina. Her lips shone in the morning light, not with color but she'd still put something shiny on them.

He pulled his eyes from her mouth, giving himself a little shake. His blood ran a little hotter and warmth crawled up his neck when she didn't look away from him either.

They'd shared a few lunches together, and he liked talking to her. But he'd been so wrapped up in the butterfly, he—

He coughed as a horrifying thought entered his mind. Had he been so wrapped up in that blasted cowgirl boot on his mantel that he'd missed a perfectly wonderful woman standing right in front of him?

"Come on, then," Trina said, almost like a real Texas cowgirl. She extended her hand toward Sabrina, and Cal saw his daughter's hesitation.

"You go on." He crouched low in front of her, placing himself between Sabrina and Trina. "She'll bring you on back to the cabin when it's time for lunch, and I promised I'd make your favorite, remember?"

Sabrina's hesitation ebbed away beneath her smile. "All right." She threw her arms around Cal and he hung on, his heart melting at the tiny touch from a tiny human.

"All right," he repeated as she stepped back and he stood up. He nodded toward Trina, and Sabrina latched their hands together.

Cal purposely kept his eyes on the ground, his emotion over having Sabrina on the ranch with him so overwhelming. Brynn patted his bicep and walked away, and Cal gathered up his courage to look at Trina.

Attraction and desire glittered in her eyes the way the sun danced on water. Cal stared right back, the draw between them that had been there since the first moment he'd met her in the lobby of Bowman's Breeds.

For some reason, he wondered if that was the first time they'd really met.

She ducked her head and tucked her too-short hair

behind her ear. "Let's go, Sabrina." She went down the aisle, letting Sabrina skip ahead of her.

Cal turned away, his chest laboring to hold a decent breath for longer than a moment.

"So you like her, huh?" Brynn said, sidling up to Cal.

"What? No." Cal pressed his hat further onto his head. "Well, I'm over at the ranch today. Text me if you need me."

He started to walk away when Brynn called, "You have to check on Grand Junction and Honeybee."

"Yeah, of course."

He detoured around the bend in the U and went down to the very end, where the two healing horses had been bunking together. Grand Junction greeted him at the door, hardly a limp in his movement at all.

They were healing well, and Cal jotted a few notes on their care sheets so Brynn would know to keep giving them the medicine and exercising them with care. Then he got the heck out of there before he went in search of Trina and demanded to know if she was the monarch butterfly he'd danced with.

He hadn't brought up the boot again, hadn't asked her if she'd gone to the dance again, hadn't perpetuated the conversation about Libby. She'd had a panic attack last time he'd asked, and he didn't need a repeat of that.

The week went quickly, with only silence on his phone. Libby didn't call. She didn't text. Cal didn't have her number, and he didn't want to come off as desperate.

But as the week ended, and another one started, the taste of need filled his mouth.

He needed to know who the butterfly was. Needed to see her again. Talk to her. And in his fantasies, he kissed her.

Cal felt like he'd lost his mind. He didn't fantasize about women. At least he hadn't in years. He worked with horses, was content, and spoiled his daughter on the weekends.

When he dropped her off at Petra's on Sunday night, Cal asked, "Can I take her to my brother's for Thanksgiving? She wants to see if he still has that German shepherd that can give high five."

"We have a big event here at the restaurant," Petra said, standing in the doorway and not allowing him entrance. He didn't need to go inside to know what it looked like. The stench of new upholstery wafted out to him, and he wondered how much she'd spent replacing items that didn't need to be replaced this time.

Her shopaholic tendencies were more of a hoarding sickness, despite what she claimed, and she'd bankrupted Cal before filing for divorce and moving back to the apartment behind the restaurant her parents owned.

Cal had been forced to sell everything he had to pay the credit card bills, all the foolishness in the world landing on his shoulders. He'd left his life in Hill Country behind and followed Petra north to the Texas Panhandle.

He'd managed to get a job at Three Rivers Ranch, only

The Curse of February Fourteenth

an hour from the restaurant, and the dissolution of their marriage had been taken care of swiftly.

Sometimes a blip of sadness stole through him, but most of the time, he knew he was better off without her. He wasn't sure if she felt the same, but she seemed to be able to go to work and take care of herself and Sabrina.

His daughter showed up with clean clothes and hair, and Petra's hoarding didn't extend to garbage or expired food. Cal was thankful for that, and he prayed for his daughter's safety and well-being constantly.

"Maybe she can miss the event for a year," Cal said coolly. "Just think, she won't be underfoot while you're baking."

Petra looked as if she never got outside, with skin as pale as onion skins. A flicker of the woman he'd met at a rodeo event in Idaho emerged, and he grinned.

"I think she'd like to go to Austin," Petra said, brushing back her blonde hair.

Cal gave her his best smile, and the corners of Petra's mouth twitched upward. For a moment, he saw the family they'd been and the family they could've been if not for her mental illnesses and her refusal to address them.

"Bye, Daddy." Sabrina wrapped her arms around Cal's waist and hugged him tight. He patted her back and bent down when she backed up.

"You gonna be sleepin' good tonight, baby?" he asked.

She put both hands on the sides of his face and peered

right into his eyes. Eyes so like his that his heart twisted and ached. "I'll be sleepin' fine, Daddy."

He nodded once, wishing with everything inside him that his life were different. That he didn't have to leave her here. He felt like this every weekend, and he knew what it took to tear himself away from Sabrina, make the lonely walk down the dirt driveway to his truck, and get himself back to the ranch that had saved him.

So he did exactly that, sure in the knowledge that if Sabrina was scared, or uncomfortable, or worried, or anything, she'd have said she didn't think she'd be able to sleep that night.

It was a game he'd invented since the day she could talk, one he'd wanted to establish so she could let him know discreetly if something wasn't right at her mother's house.

He returned to his cabin. His clean, nothing out of place, minimalist cabin, wondering if Sabrina felt as out of place here as he did in Petra's mess.

Someone knocked on the door before Cal could even kick off his boots. He knew it would be the matron of the ranch before he even opened the door. Sure enough, Squire's honey-blonde wife stood on the front porch.

"Come on over for dinner, Cal," she said, smiling as she folded her arms and cocked her hip. "I have those ridged potato chips you like, and Pete is making his guacamole as we speak."

Cal leaned against the door, unsure about if he wanted

to go over to the homestead and be with people. People with families, the way he used to be. But he also knew he'd go, because he couldn't pass up Pete's homemade guac.

Kelly gave him a look that said she knew his weaknesses and she'd expressly exploited them. She grinned and nodded toward the boot sitting on the mantel. "What's that?"

Cal straightened and settled against the other side of the doorframe to block the offending object. "Nothing."

Kelly narrowed her eyes, her mind definitely sparking, questions piling up. She turned without saying anything more until she reached the gravel path at the bottom of his steps. "I'll ask Squire."

Cal launched himself out of the cabin. "Don't do that, Miss Kelly."

"Then you better tell me yourself."

"Why? So *you* can tell Squire?"

"Either way, we're going to find out."

Cal sighed, because she was right. And maybe he could get some help on his side and finally figure out who his mysterious monarch butterfly was.

Chapter Six

"I have to quit." Trina paced in the apartment while Libby simply continued to paint her fingernails an unsavory shade of yellow.

"I mean, I have to quit." She threw her arms up in the air. She'd spent a week with Cal's daughter for a shadow, and Sabrina was a cute little girl, quiet like her father, and an absolute delight to waste hours with.

Trina had never given much thought to having children. Tennis always came first. Always. Until she didn't want it to anymore, and then Carlos had insisted.

Why hadn't he just let her quit while she was on top? That was all she'd ever wanted, and he'd taken it from her —and then found another brunette to kiss while she was still getting up at five o'clock in the morning and hitting balls when she wanted to sleep in and start a life beyond tennis.

Her emotion surged to the top of her head, clouding her thoughts, and she glanced up as if seeking divine help, a sob wrenching through her throat.

"You don't have to quit," Libby said in a monotone voice, the same way she had at least half a dozen times before.

Trina swallowed her feelings, tried to stuff them way down deep where no one would see them, or hear them. "You said you'd find out who the monarch butterfly was."

She glanced up, her hazel eyes sparking. "I did." A wicked smile curved her lips.

"You can't tell him."

"I've sworn up and down that I won't. We pinky-promised."

"Has he called you?"

"In the thirty minutes since you asked last?" Libby made a big show of checking her phone. "Nope. No calls from Cal Hodgkins." She went back to painting her nails. "I don't know why you just don't tell him who you are. It's obvious you like him."

Trina *did* like him—and that was the problem. She couldn't go getting involved with a man. And not just any man. A *cowboy* with a *child*.

She shook her head, wondering how one dance had led her to this mess. What would he think when she never wanted to go home for holidays? How could she possibly ever take him back to her house in the hills?

It's not a house, she chastised herself. It's a freaking

The Curse of February Fourteenth

mansion, with an entire room for your trophies and cups and plates....

She sighed and sank into a chair across from Libby. "Sorry," she said as she jostled the table and Libby threw her a dirty look.

"Tell me why I don't have to quit." Everything in Trina was urging her to run, and run fast. Far. Turn her back on Three Rivers and find some other small town to live in.

But this was the fourth place she'd tried, and she was starting to learn that no matter where she went, she'd still be Katrina Salisbury, former number one women's tennis player in the world, who had a public break-up with her boyfriend-slash-trainer and disappeared.

Maybe it was time to face who she was. Stay, and figure out how to *be* who she wanted to be going forward.

She put her head in her hands. She'd faced down formidable opponents before. Competitors who made her nervous, who hit the ball so hard she couldn't get to it on the court.

But she wasn't that person anymore. Maybe it was time to find a new version of herself. A newer, *better* version of herself.

"You don't have to quit, because he likes you. He *wants* to find you." She capped the nail polish and blew on her nails. "You should march into his cabin tomorrow morning and say, 'That's my boot. I danced with you. I *looooove* you.'" She giggled and Trina rolled her eyes.

"I've known the man for two weeks."

"Sometimes you know when you first set eyes on someone," she said.

Trina didn't believe in love at first sight. Never had. Didn't really have a lot of romantic bones in her body, unless she wanted to count her lifelong love affair with tennis.

She sighed and closed her eyes, the moment she'd met Cal playing through her mind. So she'd been abnormally attracted to him, drawn physically across the dance floor until she stood chest to chest with him.

Something had sizzled and crackled between them during the four-minute dance they'd shared, and—

"I'm afraid," she whispered, realizing why she'd run from him that night on the dance floor. She didn't want him to know who she was, and fear had gripped her. Gripped her hard enough to induce her flight response.

"What?" Libby switched her attention from her nails to Trina.

"I have to tell you something." Trina's heart wailed, trembled, flopped in her chest. "How familiar with women's tennis are you?"

"Women's tennis?"

With that comment, Trina knew Three Rivers was the perfect place for her to build a life outside of tennis. Knew she didn't want to leave simply because she was afraid.

"Open up your laptop," she said. "I'll show you."

Libby complied, and Trina Googled herself, getting

pages and pages of pictures and articles in less than half a second. She wanted to delete them all.

No, you don't, she told herself. And she didn't. Not really. What she'd wanted—to leave tennis on her terms—had been taken from her.

Taking a deep breath and slowly releasing it, she turned the computer back to Libby. "That's me."

Libby stared at the screen, her eyes wide and curious. "Professional tennis...number one in the world...." She looked up, surprise and shock in her expression. "You were number one in the world?"

"For sixty-four consecutive months." Trina ran her hands through her short locks, hating them. She hated the color too. It looked so yellow to her, nowhere near a natural blonde.

"I don't—ohhh."

So she'd found the pictures of Carlos. Carlos and Trina. Then Carlos and Amara. Then Carlos and Giselle.

"No wonder you paid six month's rent up front." Libby wore the same look in her eye that everyone did once they figured out she had money. A lot of money.

Libby returned to the computer to get some more juicy gossip. "This was months ago," she said after only a few seconds. She leaned away from the laptop. "And you've only been in town for a few weeks." She didn't wear any judgment in her face, and when she asked, "Where have you been?" it wasn't with any ill intentions.

"Bouncing around," Trina said. She laid her head back in her arms. "And I'm tired. I just want to stay here."

"Oh my stars. You were just thinking about running again," Libby said. "Weren't you?"

Trina nodded, her chin wobbling as her emotion got the better of her. She steeled her nerves and buried her feelings, the way she'd been doing since the day she picked up a tennis racquet.

"You don't want Cal to know."

"I don't want anyone to know."

Libby closed the laptop instead of staring at another article, analyzing more pictures. Trina appreciated that, and she gave her roommate a weak smile.

"I don't see how telling him you're the monarch butterfly has anything to do with your tennis career."

Trina tried to explain it in a way that wouldn't hurt Libby's feelings. "People…treat me differently once they know I've won Wimbledon."

"Twice," Libby said with a grin.

Trina blinked and then a laugh burst out of her mouth. Libby joined in, and Trina released all the pent-up emotions she'd bottled up and carried around with her for the past six months.

"So I'm texting Cal." Libby lunged for her phone while terror gripped Trina's heart.

"I'll tell him," she said. "Let me tell him."

But how she was going to do that, she had no idea. But

her promise got Libby to lower the phone, and Trina felt like she'd just bought herself a tiny window of time.

She didn't tell Cal on Monday. He was in a very bad mood, and she even skipped eating lunch with him to give him some space.

She didn't tell him on Tuesday, as he didn't seem to be anywhere on-site that day. She found out on Wednesday that he'd gone to Amarillo with Pete and Squire and Brynn to a horse auction. They didn't return until Thursday afternoon, and then it was all hands on deck as they unloaded six new horses.

Friday, Miss Kelly fed everyone on the property, including all the employees at Courage Reins, the equine therapy clinic, and Brynn's place.

Trina didn't want to go, but her other option of dining alone with Cal while she stared at her black cowgirl boot was out, so she went.

Cal came over to her immediately. "Hey, there." He gave her a grin that rivaled the sun in brightness and heat. His fingers brushed against hers, causing a breath to stick in her lungs. So many people milled about, talking, laughing, and going up the stairs to a huge deck where Kelly and Squire stood serving everyone in the line.

"Do they do this often?" Trina asked, sticking close to Cal as he hung back from everyone else.

"Every couple of months." He glanced up to the deck and back to Trina. "You want to take our chili back to my cabin?"

Relief rushed through her. "Absolutely."

His grin made a reappearance. "Great." He slid his fingers in between hers and held on with a tight squeeze. "I've missed you this week." He released her hand, leaving her skin cold and her muscles, tendons, and bones tingling.

Cal moved up the stairs, leaving Trina to stare after him. He missed her?

Libby's voice practically shrieked in Trina's ears. *Tell him. Tell him today!*

He glanced back at her and gestured for her to come through the line with him. She joined him, because the country version of Trina Salisbury wanted to.

By the time they escaped the crowd and made it into the silence of his cabin, Trina needed some painkillers and an injection of patience. She groaned as she sat at his kitchen table.

"Rough week?"

"Rough lunch," she said.

He placed a plate of butter between them. "What do you mean?"

"I don't like crowds."

"Ah." He nodded and scooped up a bite of chili. "I don't like tomatoes."

"How are you eating chili then?" She giggled as she

The Curse of February Fourteenth

filled her spoon with tomatoes, black beans, and beef. "I mean, it's tomato-based."

"I'll eat them in soups and stews." He took another bite, as if to prove his point.

"What else don't you like?"

"Summer."

"Summer?" She stared at him. "Everyone loves summer."

"You haven't lived through one in Texas, obviously." He grinned as he spread butter on his cornbread.

"I haven't. But I've...traveled all over the world. Been in a lot of hot places." Sometimes during the worst times of the year. He should try London in July.

"Traveled all over the world, huh?" He watched her from under the brim of that sexy hat, and Trina glanced toward the boot still sitting in his living room. It had been moved since the last time she'd been here, which meant he looked at it, picked it up, thought about it often.

"Yeah, in a...previous life." She took another bite, everything inside her on fire, which had nothing to do with the jalapenos in the chili. She put her spoon down. "Look, I have to tell you something."

"Shoot." He didn't seem worried about whatever she was going to say, but the words got lodged in her throat. Surprising, as she hadn't been able to come up with any words. Not really.

"I'm, well, when we met—"

"Cal?" A man whose head nearly hit the top of the

doorframe as he leaned inside knocked after he'd spoken. "Shirley Temple is throwin' a fit, and she's gashed her leg on her stall. Brynn needs you."

He glanced at Trina, noticing her for the first time. "Oh, hello, ma'am." He ducked his head and retreated out of the cabin as fast as he'd come.

Cal was already on his way toward the door. "Stay as long as you like," he called over his shoulder. "I'll find you later."

He was gone just as fast, leaving Trina to whisper, "We met at the masked ball. We danced one magical, beautiful dance before I freaked out and ran away."

She looked at the boot. "That boot is mine."

There. She'd said it. Too bad no one was around to hear it.

Chapter Seven

The weather worsened the deeper into November the days went. Trina came over for lunch everyday. Sometimes Cal entered his cabin to find her already there, sometimes seated at the table as she used his microwave to heat something from home. Sometimes curled into the couch as she ate a peanut butter sandwich. And once, he'd walked in to find her holding that black cowgirl boot and whispering something.

He'd broken the physical barrier between them, and if she sat on the couch, he sat next to her. If she ate at the table, he ate across from her. He held her hand as they walked down the gravel path, and his dreams started to match his daydreams, all of them featuring a kiss with Trina.

One day, the week before Thanksgiving, they strolled out behind the cabins, enjoying the sunlight even though the wind tried to chase it away. She claimed to love the open land, the wildness of it, and Cal had started to appreciate it more.

He'd learned she didn't like social media, or athletes, or pomegranates. She did love a big juicy hamburger and rising early enough to catch the sunrise.

They usually filled their limited time with chatter, but today, they both stayed silent. At least until she said, "You go to church, right?"

Surprise lifted his eyebrows. "Yes."

"Every week?"

"Most every week, yeah."

"And you take Sabrina."

"Yes."

Trina paused and looked up at him with scared eyes. Her tension radiated in the space between them. "Could I go with you this week?"

Cal grinned. "Of course." He released her hand and tucked her close to his body, guiding her back to a walk. "Have you been to church before?"

"No."

"Not even as a little girl?"

She shook her head, her hesitation swirling with the wind. He'd suspected she had a past she didn't want him to know about; she'd dropped enough hints for him to guess. Traveled all over the world. Never been to church. And her hair had started growing in and it wasn't naturally the color of the butterscotch discs his grandmother kept in a bowl on her front table.

It was dark.

Cal had all but given up on his monarch butterfly. He'd texted Libby a few times over the past few weeks, but she either ignored him or answered with a terse *Don't know yet.*

He wasn't sure he cared to find the other woman. He had Trina right next to him, and he found her interesting and beautiful.

He hadn't kissed a woman in a while, wasn't quite sure how much courage it took, didn't know how to tell if the moment was right.

But he paused and turned toward her. "Trina," he said, his voice low and almost getting whisked away by the weather. "I sure like you."

She tilted her head back to look up into his face, a smile filling hers. "I sure like you right on back."

He cupped her face in his palms and lowered his mouth toward hers slowly, painfully slowly, giving her a chance to escape if she wanted to.

She didn't want to, because she stretched up to kiss him too, and when his lips met hers, an explosion of heat shot through him.

He handled her gently, carefully, exploring her lips until he knew every centimeter of them. It was easily the best kiss of his life, and his heart galloped like a herd of wild mustangs by the time he pulled back.

She gazed up at him, pure wonder and...adoration in her expression. She smiled and ducked her head as she wrapped him in an embrace that he could feel along his ribs long after she let go.

* * *

On Sunday morning, Cal stood in the bathroom, supervising Sabrina as she brushed her teeth. "Get all the way to the back ones," he said.

"Mom says they'll all fall out anyway," Sabrina said around a mouth of foamy toothpaste.

"Still have to take care of 'em," he said, hoping his voice sounded nonchalant and not like he was mentally cursing Petra for pardoning poor hygiene simply because those teeth would fall out later.

She finished and jumped down from the stool he kept in the bathroom cupboard. "Can we go riding after church today?"

"Not today, baby. We're...." His throat closed. He wasn't aware of Petra dating anyone since the divorce, and he had no idea how to explain Trina to his six-year-old. "We're stopping by Trina's house to pick her up for church. Remember Trina?"

"The horse feeder."

"Right," Cal said. "She's comin' to church for the first time today."

Sabrina just looked at him, waiting for more. But Cal

knew it had taken some serious bravery for Trina to ask him about church.

"We'll come back here and have lunch with her," he said, hoping that was a good enough explanation. "You'll probably get to see her in the next few days while you're here, before we go to Uncle Kyle's for Thanksgiving."

Sabrina didn't argue or seem upset. He loaded her up and drove into town, finding the apartment building around the corner from the bank easily. "Scootch on over into the middle, baby. I'll go grab her, and she can sit by the window."

Her front door opened before Cal could get there, and Libby emerged first. "Cal Hodgkins." The way she always said his first and last name put this awkward air between them. He smiled at her anyway.

"Libby Larsen." He glanced behind her to find Trina.

"She didn't own a dress, so we did the best we could." Libby turned to face the door and called, "Come on out, Trina."

Cal licked his lips, unsure of what he'd see when Trina finally appeared, his heart running away with his imagination.

Trina emerged wearing a black skirt that probably went to Libby's ankles. But on Trina, it hit mid-calf, revealing a pair of blue-as-denim flats. Her blouse was the color of the sunflowers that grew wild in the fields around the ranch, and it hung a little awkwardly off her narrow shoulders.

She took his breath away. One hundred percent left him breathless, the same way the monarch butterfly at the masked ball had. He found himself moving toward her and sweeping her into his arms, forgetting or not caring that Libby stood a dozen feet away and that his daughter was likely watching from the truck.

"You are beautiful," he whispered in her ear just before placing his lips against her soft skin there.

She trembled slightly in his arms and he regained his composure long enough to put the proper distance between them. He tucked her hand in his and turned back to Libby, who wore a giddy look on her face. She even bounced up and down on the balls of her feet and clapped her hands.

"You guys are so cute together. You're right though, Trina. You can't wear heels with him."

Trina looked up at him and smiled. "You look nice."

"Thank you, sunflower."

"Sunflower?"

He reached over and fingered the blouse, pulling it slightly off her shoulder. He stared at the newly exposed skin, his thoughts bursting into fantasies he couldn't play out right now. "This reminds me of sunflowers," he said through a parched throat.

"Well, your hat reminds me of coal, but you don't hear me using that as a term of endearment."

"So no Sunflower."

She shook her head, a playful smile toying with her

mouth. Cal wanted to lean down and wipe that small smirk from her lips by kissing her. He opened the passenger door of the truck, kissless.

"What about baby?" he asked.

Sabrina looked over. "Yeah, Daddy?"

Trina cocked her eyebrows. "No baby."

Cal chuckled as he helped her into the truck, waving to Libby as she climbed into her own car.

"Hi, Trina," Sabrina said as Cal swung the door closed. He went around the front of the truck, his eyes never leaving the two ladies in his truck. They were both smiling, and Trina said something that made Sabrina laugh.

Cal's heart squeezed out an extra beat, then two. Could this be his reality long-term? Could he build a stable family unit for his daughter?

If he could, he knew one thing: He wanted to do the rebuilding with Trina.

Go slow, he coached himself. *Be cautious. Every decision you make impacts three lives.* His. Sabrina's. And as much as he didn't want to admit it, Petra's. Her life was eternally intertwined with his, whether he liked it or not.

One of his father's mantras came to mind. Make good choices, then you only have to make them once.

Cal wanted to do better than he'd done in the past when it came to choosing a wife. He couldn't believe he was thinking about Trina like that after only five weeks, but there the thought sat, right in the middle of his brain.

His parents would be at his brother's for Thanksgiving too, and Cal couldn't wait to see everyone. Maybe they'd be able to help him make sense of his jumbled feelings, help him iron them flat and examine them.

As he drove toward the church and parked, his thoughts turned heavenward, and he pleaded for help. Help with Sabrina. Help to know what to do and say with Trina to make her first day at church meaningful and enjoyable.

"All right, ladies," he said as he took the truck out of gear. "Let's go."

He got out of the truck first and waved for Sabrina to slide out on his side. He held her hand as he went around to help Trina, who also kept a firm hold on his fingers.

"You okay?" he asked.

"No one's going to...well, I don't really know what people will do."

He chuckled and lifted her wrist to his lips. "Expect a lot of staring. But that's about it."

"Staring," she mumbled. "Great."

Chapter Eight

Trina was sure most of the staring landed on her and Cal's joined hands. He walked between her and Sabrina, and Trina felt like she was on display.

She'd lived her whole life like that, but she still didn't like the squiggly feeling in her stomach or the way her jaw muscles ached from holding her face so still for so long.

He led her to a pew on the left side in the back. "We sit back here," he said, ushering Sabrina into the row first. "Because Bri likes to leave as soon as the choir sings the last song."

"Do people normally stay later?" Trina asked, admiring Cal as he helped his daughter get all the way over so there was room for all of them.

"Some like to mingle, chat with each other, that kind of thing."

Trina would like to leave as soon as the last note sounded in the hall also.

"And the pastor comes out and speaks to everyone," Cal said. "We almost always beat him out."

"Sounds great," Trina said, not knowing she'd need to "mingle" and "speak with the pastor."

They'd arrived early, and Trina gazed around the chapel, awed by the rich wood, the high ceilings, and the beauty of the morning light spilling through the huge windows in front of her and behind her.

An overwhelming sense of gratitude filled her, reminding her of the many things in her life she had. Maybe it was the Thanksgiving season, or maybe she was finally figuring out who she was, but she closed her eyes and sent the simplest prayer toward the rafters.

Thank you.

Her phone buzzed against her palm and she flipped it over and opened her eyes to *Mom* on the screen.

She smiled, probably for the first time, at the text.

Missing you today.

Another one came right after it.

How are you?

Really great, Trina texted back, the smallest of smiles forming on her face. She felt the weight of Cal's eyes on her phone, and she tilted it toward him. "My mother."

He lifted his arm and draped it around Trina's shoulders, making her feel warm and wanted. She'd never felt small next to a man, but he made her feel that way—in a very good way. A way like he'd take care of her, protect her, love her no matter what happened.

Why so great? her mom asked.

Trina hunched her shoulders as her thumbs flew across the screen. *Just that the job is going great, and I've made some friends.*

So are you going to stay wherever you are?

Trina glanced up as a man announced, "Brothers and Sisters, welcome to our Sabbath Day worship." He wore a bright smile and had a trustworthy face. Trina liked him instantly, even from this distance.

"That's Miss Kelly's cousin's husband." Cal's lips practically tasted her ear he leaned so close.

Shivers cascaded across her shoulders. She hadn't felt so giddy about a man in all of her thirty-three years. "I don't even know how to follow that," Trina whispered back.

Her phone forgotten, Trina focused on the way the choir filled the entire chapel with music as rousing as it was spiritual. And Trina felt something zing along her neck, down her spine, all the way into her toes.

She didn't know what it was, but she liked the way it made her feel more powerful than she currently did. She liked the way she felt like she could fail and be okay. She liked the way she felt like she could change her life if she wanted to.

And she wanted to.

Trina picked up her phone and typed Yes, Mom. I'm going to stay where I am.

Right where she was, right next to Cal.

She snuggled deeper into his chest and he squeezed her shoulder and placed a kiss on her head. She'd experienced lazy days like this before—right after a big win, when she was home alone, drinking hot chocolate and ordering her favorite kind of pizza.

Today felt like that—like she could wear sweats and forget about makeup and no one would care. That whoever she ran into would accept her for who she was.

The feeling lasted all the way out to the ranch, where Cal made grilled cheese sandwiches and opened a couple of cans of tomato soup. He filled them with milk while Sabrina told Trina about their upcoming trip to Austin.

"Daddy says I can sleep with the other kids in the bunk beds."

"Where do you normally sleep?" Trina asked, settling on the couch and keeping one eye on Cal in the kitchen. A man who could cook…definitely sexy.

"With Daddy. But he says I'm getting too old, and Uncle Kyle said there's room with the cousins." Sabrina pushed her shoes off her feet and sat right next to Trina.

"When's the last time you saw your Uncle Kyle?"

Sabrina wore a blank look and shrugged. So not in a while. Trina didn't know what that said about Cal—probably that he had a very busy job and didn't visit his brother very often. She didn't need to read too much into it.

The Curse of February Fourteenth

"Lunch," Cal called, and Trina followed Sabrina into the kitchen, slightly less skip in her step. He'd told her about his two sisters and one brother. She'd mentioned her family to him briefly. He'd given the details of his marriage and divorce, including that his ex-wife had some mental disabilities and more shoes than anyone should ever own. Still, her heart had gone out to him when he'd detailed the day the divorce papers had come.

Valentine's Day. Though he'd been expecting the divorce papers, no one wanted a county representative with a large envelope with all the wrong papers inside for Valentine's Day.

Even though the story was sad, Trina had enjoyed the sound of his voice mingling with the breeze, the openness of the land here as they'd walked. Cal didn't seem to like being caged by walls either, so they at least had that in common.

When they finished eating, Cal cleared the dishes but just left them in the sink. "Who wants to go for a walk?"

Trina rose and brushed her hands together. "I do."

"Can we take the barn dogs?" Sabrina asked.

"Go see if they're there."

Sabrina skipped toward the front door. Cal watched her, a smile lighting his whole face. "They'll be there. They just lay around on Sundays."

"Barn dogs?"

"Oh, Squire's got a couple of dogs he uses to help

round up the cattle. Well, more than a couple, but these two were born in the barn, and they like it there."

"What kind of dogs?"

"Blue heelers, like mine."

Trina glanced around. "You have dogs?"

Cal blinked at her. "I have two dogs."

"Where?" She seriously had never seen a dog here before. "How did I not know this?"

"They hang out around the ranch," he said. "You never saw the dog food bowls on the front porch?"

She glanced at the boot, still stuck in place like a horrible painting that someone had glued up and Cal couldn't remove no matter how hard he tried. "No, I've never seen the dog food bowls on the porch."

"Blitz and Bits," he said. "They're mine, but they roam around. They help with the round-up too."

"Do you help with the round-up?"

He swept one arm around her and brought her close. "This may surprise you, but I'm not just a veterinary technician. I rode the rodeo circuit for a year and worked ranches while I finished school."

"That isn't a definitive answer."

He chuckled and ducked his head to place a kiss on her cheek. "Yes, I help with the round-up too. I'm Squire's Number Two, remember? And he has fifty thousand head of cattle that need looking after."

Trina's head spun with the vastness of what they did at the ranch. She had no idea what it took to keep that many animals alive and healthy. What kind of chores the cowhands had to face everyday. The finances for an operation as large as this.

"Found 'em." Sabrina stuck her head into the house. "Let's go."

"Let's go," Cal echoed, nudging Trina toward the door. Once on the porch, he leaned into the railing and whistled through his teeth. The shrill sound seemed to go on forever, and it pitched up for the last second.

Two gray streaks came around the corner, becoming more dog-shaped the closer they got. They bounded up the steps to Cal, their tails wagging and their tongues lagging out of their mouths.

"See? Blitz and Bits." He leaned over and scrubbed them down, the adoration for his dogs evident in his treatment of them as he told them what good dogs they were and that they needed baths.

"Can I bathe 'em, Daddy?"

"No, baby," he told Sabrina. "Ranch dogs don't actually get baths. We can spray 'em with the hose after we walk, if you want."

Sabrina didn't seem upset by his denial, and she skipped between the cabins, all four dogs trotting after her. Trina wasn't sure how she felt about the blue heelers, but when Cal captured her hand in his, they disappeared from her mind.

There was only Cal and the delicious heat from his touch.

"What are you doing for Thanksgiving?" he asked.

"Libby invited me to her parents' in Oklahoma City."

Several paces passed before he said, "She just learned how to skip," and nodded toward his daughter.

Trina watched Sabrina as she literally skipped from one flower to a clump of brown grasses, then over to one of the dogs. "She's great."

"I think so, but I'm pretty biased." He squeezed her hand. "What did you think of church?"

"I liked it," she said, genuine happiness bubbling up inside her. "I really liked it."

"That's great."

Trina felt like the pieces of her new self were out there, swimming just beyond her reach. She just needed to grab them all and make them fit together. Maybe one of the pieces was the care of her spirit, something she'd never really done.

"So you said you needed to tell me something," Cal said, his voice a bit on the guarded side. "The other day at lunch. Something about when we met."

Trina's mind went from calm and relaxed to frenzied in a single breath. She searched her mind for what she'd said, but nothing came. She didn't want to ruin this perfect day with her confession about who she was. At the same time, she was tired of living with the weight of keeping her identity a secret.

"Trina?"

"What do you remember about when we met?"

Cal gazed at the horizon. "I remember you were beautiful. Took my breath away."

A kernel of warmth pushed against the truth she was withholding from him. She, more than anyone, knew that secrets had a cost, that they were never free.

"I remember thinking I needed to ask you for help," she said.

"Help?"

"With the horses."

"I don't follow."

"I...." Trina cleared her throat, searching for the words. "I'm a California city girl, Cal. I have no experience with horses."

He slitted his eyes and looked at her out of the corner of them. "You do now."

"I suppose that's true."

"Brynn has never said anything negative about you."

"That's because she's really kind." Trina giggled but it came out more strangled than anything else. "I watched videos on the Internet to learn how to saddle a horse. I wasn't even sure what a stable was."

Cal said nothing, and the space between them turned charged. "Bri," he called after his daughter. "Don't go that way." He released Trina's hand and stalked away. He scooped up his daughter and their laughter filled the sky.

Still, Trina felt sure he was upset with her. She slowed and fell further behind, enjoying the time to herself the way she always had. At the same time, she didn't want to live with Libby forever, and she didn't want to live alone either. She hadn't lived alone as an adult ever. She always had security, or an assistant, or her parents.

She drew in a deep breath and watched as Cal turned back to her. Something had definitely changed in his demeanor. In the past, Trina wouldn't have cared. She'd have restrung her racquet, toughened up her mental game, and gone out there to crush the competition.

But this wasn't tennis, and Cal wasn't her opponent.

And she didn't like the person she used to be.

So it was time to do something different, be someone different.

Chapter Nine

Cal wasn't great at bottling his emotions to deal with later. He wasn't sure why his annoyance switch had been flipped when Trina had mentioned that she'd taken a job she had no right to even apply for.

He'd hurried away from her before she could discover his frustration, but it hung like a scent on the air, and she wasn't stupid. Quite the opposite, in fact.

You like her too much, he told himself for the tenth time since picking her up that morning. Since he'd kissed her, he'd thought about little else. He wanted to see her in the morning, before he brushed his teeth. See her puttering around the kitchen at lunchtime, heating up a container of last night's leftovers. See her in the last moments before he closed his eyes and fell asleep.

Sure, the relationship had progressed fast, but Cal was old enough to know what he liked and what he wanted.

And he liked Trina and wanted to be with her.

"Hey," she said, approaching him with long, sure strides. "What's wrong?"

"Wrong?" He set Sabrina down on the ground and patted her back, hoping she'd run after Blitz and Bits. She did, leaving him to speak with Trina in private.

"I can tell you're upset." She folded her arms and looked him straight in the eye.

And boy, if that didn't make his blood run hotter. "I appreciate hearing things straight up," he said, finally realizing what had bothered him so much about what she'd said. "I don't like liars."

Her eyes flashed. "You think I'm lying?"

"I have a feeling," he said. "I have for a while. You're… evasive about certain things."

She clenched her arms across her chest and looked away.

"Like that," he said. "I've seen you do that several times. When I asked you about your family. About college." Another light bulb went on in his brain. "Pretty much anything in your life that happened before you arrived here."

"I don't want the life I had before I got here. Did you ever think of that?"

Cal's heart cinched. "What happened?" he asked, his voice low in both pitch and volume so he wouldn't scare her away. "Why don't you want that life?"

"Wasn't the one I wanted."

"Is that what you're doing here? Starting over?"

"Yes." She swept the horizon before focusing on him again. "And I've learned a lot on the job. Brynn's taught me a lot. I've been able to do everything she's asked. I work hard, and I'm smart, and I—"

"I know, Trina." Regret filled him and he flitted his fingers toward hers, brushing the tips against her wrist.

"I didn't lie," she said. "About the job. She called me and asked me if I could start on Monday. I said yes, and she said the job was mine."

Cal's eyes widened. "She didn't ask you anything about horses?"

"Not a thing."

He put his arms around her and pulled her the one step into his arms. She remained stiff, unyielding, exactly what he expected from someone as headstrong and beautiful as Trina. He'd enjoyed their walks through the countryside so much, loved telling her about his brother and sisters, his ex-wife, his daughter.

So he'd revealed more than she had. Didn't mean she'd lied, and he felt bad for accusing her of such things.

"I'm sorry," he whispered. "My—Petra taught me not to trust anything anyone says. I'm cautious, that's all."

She finally relaxed against his chest, her arms coming up around his back. Nothing felt as good as holding Trina, and he slipped a little further down the slope toward love.

Fear overtook his thoughts. Everything was moving so fast. Too fast. He'd only met this woman a few weeks ago, and yet he'd been entertaining thoughts of her living with him in the cabin on the ranch and tying ribbons into his daughter's hair before church.

He told himself that he didn't have to get married next week just because he liked Trina. At the same time, Cal wasn't one to wait around when he knew what he wanted.

"My parents don't know where I am," she said, her breath warming through the fabric of his shirt and infecting his skin.

He pulled back, acknowledging the very vulnerable thing she'd just said. He put his fingers under her chin and lifted her face toward his so he could see her eyes. Agony lived there, and Cal wanted nothing more than to take it away. Fix everything in her life, the way she seemed to have fixed him.

She stretched up and touched the tip of her nose against his, her mouth half an inch from his. "Why haven't you told them?" he asked, their breath mingling together. Every cell in his body tingled in anticipation, and still she didn't kiss him.

"I—I—"

He ran his thumb along her bottom lip, a growl starting low in his stomach. She finally grazed his mouth with hers, leaving him hungry and wanting more. So much more.

"Cal," she started, and hearing his name in her heated, husky voice sent a pulse straight through him. "I'm not who you think I am."

The Curse of February Fourteenth

He didn't care who she was. He knew who he'd gotten to know over the past month, and he liked that woman a whole lot.

"Who are you?" he asked anyway.

She claimed his mouth fully then, and he kissed her back eagerly and brought her flush against him. He thrilled at the touch of her cool fingers along his warmer neck, along his hairline, down the sides of his face.

He kissed her and kissed her, deepening their connection until he thought sure she'd push him away. But she didn't, and Cal finally got ahold of his hormones and broke the kiss. Just because it was Trina's first time at church didn't mean Cal didn't know better. He did.

He tried to calm his ragged breathing with a deep inhale, but his heart still raced like he'd just finished running a marathon.

"My name is Katrina Salisbury," she said.

"I already know that." He skated his lips along her jaw, desperate for a taste of her neck.

She gave it to him and said, "I used to be a professional tennis player."

That froze him, and he lifted his eyes to hers. "Oh?"

"A really good one. I ended the season last year at number one."

Cal pulled back, needing some additional brainpower. And he didn't seem to think very clearly with the scent of her raspberry skin so close, the tantalizing shape of her mouth distracting him so easily.

"Number one, huh?" he said. He may not have kept up with women's tennis specifically, but even he knew what it took to be number one in the world in a sport. No wonder she'd been able to pick up her work with the horses so easily. She was used to working long hours, getting up early, and getting yelled at.

Not that Brynn yelled, but still.

"Number one," she confirmed.

Cal studied Trina, trying to see her in a short tennis skirt, a racquet in her hand, her hair pulled back into a tight ponytail.

His eyes drifted to her roots. It would definitely be a dark-haired ponytail.

"Has Libby said anything else about the monarch butterfly?" he asked.

Her eyes, which had softened, turned to glass. "No." She stepped out of his arms and turned around. "I'm ready to go back." She took a few steps and paused.

Cal cursed himself for bringing up the monarch butterfly. He'd all but given up hope that Libby would find out who she was, and Trina had been a suitable replacement for her. Better, actually.

He really wanted her to be the monarch butterfly. *His* monarch butterfly, who morphed and transformed into something beautiful and majestic. Who helped him transform into someone better. Someone who deserved someone as beautiful and powerful as that butterfly-woman had been at the masked ball.

The Curse of February Fourteenth

Trina glanced back at him, tucking her short hair behind her ear as if it used to be longer.

"Sabrina," he called to his daughter. "Blitz, Bits!" He whistled through his teeth, bringing everyone back to him. "We're goin' back, baby."

"Can we have brownies and ice cream now?"

He tousled her hair, wishing his life was as easy as brownies and ice cream. "Sure thing."

Sabrina skipped ahead to where Trina stood and declared, "Daddy makes the best brownies," before continuing back toward the row of cabins in the distance.

Trina met his eye, and he wasn't sure if he should make a joke about the brownies—which came from a boxed mix—or apologize, or kiss her senseless.

One thing he did know: He needed to get rid of that boot.

* * *

CAL ONLY WORKED until lunchtime the following day, and he left Sabrina with Trina at the kitchen table, where they were playing Go Fish.

He was running into town to get a few things to take to his brother's house for Thanksgiving, namely three of Heidi's delicious pies. Since she'd opened the bakery a few years ago, she had a pie list that started on October first. Cal had learned his lesson and put his order in early. He hadn't known he was going to Austin to visit Kyle, but

Kelly had donated her two pies, so Cal was picking up two pumpkin pies and one pecan.

Heidi had even agreed to freeze them so he could get them to his brother's without any problems.

"Afternoon, ma'am," he said when it was his turn at the counter. He even swiped off his cowboy hat and ducked his head.

"Cal." She beamed up at him the way his mother would if she were there. An ache stabbed through his chest; it had been way too long since he'd visited his parents, and something sharp told him he'd need to let them know he wouldn't do that again.

"I've got your pies in the freezer there. Go on and get them."

"I need to pay." He reached for his wallet in his back pocket.

"Not this year." She grinned. "Tell your mother hello for me."

Gratitude filled Cal. "You sure?"

"Do you think I do anything I don't want to do?" She scoffed and waved his wallet away. "Squire says Sabrina is getting big."

Cal nodded, a ball of emotion in his throat. "She is," he managed to say.

"Kelly says you're dating a pretty girl." Heidi leaned into the counter though he wasn't the only one in line.

"I am," Cal said, wondering if he and Trina were dating. He hadn't taken her out to dinner, or to the movies, or anything even remotely resembling dating. But he was kissing her....

"I'll just get these pies and go, ma'am." He put his hat back on and stepped out of line so he wouldn't take up too much time. With the three boxes sitting securely next to him on the bench seat, he headed down the main drag in town so he could get back to the turnoff for the ranch.

He whistled along to the song on the radio, everything shiny and wonderful for the first time in a long time. The pies, his daughter, this trip to Kyle's, Trina.

Cal grinned and flipped on his blinker to turn right, north, and go out to the ranch.

On the left, a flash of orange caught his eye.

The thought, *a butterfly wing,* stole through his mind, a whisper as soft as smoke.

He slammed his foot on the brake pedal, his thoughts screaming *the pies! Don't ruin the pies!* He flung his arm out to catch them, saving them from sliding off the seat and splatting on the floor.

He glanced to his left, and sure enough, a set of monarch butterfly wings was walking away from him.

His heart pulsed, skipped, pumped, skidded inside his chest. He pulled off the street and left the truck running as he leapt from it. The woman was halfway down the block and walking in the opposite direction. Dozens of people lingered between them, drinking coffee or eating lunch under eaves.

Cal called, "Hey!" hoping that didn't make him into a

creeper. Several people turned toward him, but not the butterfly. He increased his pace and ignored the stares as he broke into a jog to catch the woman.

Confusion raced through him, around and around in his brain. So many things weren't right, but he couldn't process them. All he could see was those black and orange wings.

The auburn hair registered only a moment before he said, "Hey, can I ask you a...." He trailed off as Libby turned around.

She definitely hadn't been the monarch butterfly at the ball. Number one, she was much too short. Number two, her hair was the wrong color.

Cal sucked in a breath, and released it, repeating the action several times while his mind whirred. "Libby?"

"Cal," she said, omitting his last name—and sending up a red flag.

He examined the wings. "What's—who's—these are the wings that woman wore at the masked ball."

"Yes," she said. "I mean, no. I mean—"

"Libby," he said, a definite edge in his voice. "Who was that woman?"

"I swore I wouldn't tell you." She wrung her hands and glanced over her shoulder to where a couple sat eating hamburgers and tots.

The jacket Cal wore to keep the almost-December chill off his skin suddenly seemed way too warm. "So you know who she is." His voice coming out of his throat felt like he'd swallowed a large ice cube.

"I know who she is," Libby whispered, her face turning pale and her eyes widening even further.

Cal's blood thrummed through his ears so loud he almost missed it when she said, "So do you."

He stumbled back a step. "What? Who?" He only knew a handful of women in town, and he'd been spending all his time with—

"Trina?" he asked.

Hope ballooned in his chest at the same time his heart backfired. It couldn't be her. Surely she'd have said something, anything, when she'd seen her boot sitting on his mantel.

Foolishness hit him like a fist in the face, amplified when Libby said, "It was Trina." She looked like she might start crying. "She'd only been in town a few days, and she didn't have anything to wear, so she borrowed—"

Cal held up his hand and Libby muted like she was a puppet and he the master. Anger had never tasted so bitter and roared through him with the strength of an inferno, the way it was now. Not even when Petra had served him divorce papers on Valentine's Day.

He spun on his cowboy boot and marched back down the street, his fists clenched at his sides. People continued to stare, but he ignored them easily, his emotions surging and making everything but his goal invisible.

Chapter Ten

Trina felt a chill in the air and lifted her head from the trough where she'd been feeding a six-month-old horse. She didn't see anyone, but there was definitely a change coming. She'd just straightened when she heard a male voice around the corner.

She froze.

Everything paused.

Cal knows.

She took a step toward the corner and fell back. She should hide. Run now, before she had to see him.

She wanted to run.

She wanted to stay.

She wanted...Cal.

She couldn't decide.

In the end, she didn't get to decide. Cal rounded the corner, his handsome face a perfect storm of fury. He'd been walking fast, but he came to a complete standstill when he saw her.

And just like when she'd met him at the Halloween ball, this strong tether of attraction made her legs take a step toward him even though she didn't expressly tell them to. "I'm the monarch butterfly," she said. "I danced with you at the ball, and it was the single best thing I've ever done in my life."

He swallowed, his eyes this electric blue that practically shot lightning bolts at her. "I have that stupid boot on my stupid mantel, and you said nothing. Why?"

What a great question. Before, it was because she didn't want anyone to know who she was. She hadn't planned on staying in Three Rivers. Hadn't planned on finding a way to be a different person here. Definitely hadn't planned on falling in love.

She spread her arms wide and let them fall back to her sides, her emotions knotted and tangling even more. "I was afraid." Tears choked her words and narrowed her throat.

His phone went off, and he ignored it, his gaze singular on her. The ring silenced, only to start up again a few seconds later. He pulled the device from his jacket pocket, swiped on the call, and said, "Hey, baby," in the voice he saved just for his daughter.

Trina couldn't look away from him, but it didn't matter. He turned his back on her. "Yes, I'm coming. We're leaving right now." He took two steps and paused, twisting back to her.

The Curse of February Fourteenth

What more could she say? She lifted her chin, silently begging him to come sweep her into his arms and whisper that everything would be all right. The panic she'd kept at bay for a month welled right behind her lungs, edging upward, drowning her.

Did he not have anything to say? Redness colored his cheeks, and those brilliant eyes hooked hers and sang to her soul.

He turned and walked away, the echoing ring of his bootsteps on the concrete the worst sound Trina had ever endured.

"I just can't go," she told Libby later that night. "Please, Libs. Can we just drop this?" She rolled over in bed and faced the wall. Everything hurt. Her muscles, from the long day of work. Her brain, from the way her thoughts bombarded her over, and over, and over. Her heart, from the giant hole Cal had left in it with his silent abandonment.

Was this how her mom felt, the day she'd come to Trina's for lunch to find her daughter packed and gone?

Tears trickled out of her eyes and ran down her face, toward her ear. She sniffled, and the bed moved as Libby sat on it. "I don't want you to be alone."

"I'm fine," Trina said. "I like being alone." And that was the honest truth. She thrived when she was alone—at least until she'd met Cal. Tennis was a lonely game; she was the only one on the court, the only one deciding her fate.

She'd survived the past nine months on her own—at least until she'd met Cal. And Libby. And Brynn. And everyone she worked with out on the ranch.

Trina sat up. "I'm going to call my mom." She reached for her phone as Libby stood.

"I'll give you some privacy." She left, pulling the bedroom door closed behind her.

The phone only rang once before her mom said, "Trina? Where are you?"

"Mom." Trina's voice broke as she pictured the one person who'd loved her through everything. Even when she lost games. Even when she won. Even when she continued in a relationship she knew wasn't right. Even when she disappeared. Even when her name and reputation was smeared all over the Internet for everyone to see.

"Where are you? I'll come get you."

Of course she would, and Trina's tears fell. "I don't want you to come get me, Mom," she said, drawing in a deep, deep breath for strength. "I'm in Three Rivers, Texas, and I love it here. I want to make a life for myself here."

"Honey—Texas?"

"I'm so sorry, Mom," she said. "Will you tell Dad? I'm sorry I left and didn't even say anything to you."

The Curse of February Fourteenth

"It's fine," her mom said. "Over and done. We knew what you were going through."

Well, at least they thought they did. Trina hadn't told them that she'd found out about Carlos's philandering on Valentine's Day last year. She hadn't been brave enough to confront him then. The new tennis season had already started, and though she didn't really care about it, wasn't playing with her heart the way she needed to in order to win, she also wasn't a quitter.

But when he was videotaped with another woman on a questionable beach in France while she served her way to victory on the clay courts, everything had become public. She was asked about his love affair with the blonde athlete from Croatia she'd beaten in the first round during her after-match interviews, for crying out loud.

She'd left France immediately following her win, and she hadn't picked up a racquet since. And she didn't regret it.

Her parents had been there for the last five months, but Trina had suffered through the four previous months alone. She was so tired of being alone.

"You should come home for Thanksgiving," Mom said.

"I can't," Trina said automatically. "I'm working until Wednesday, and I only have Thursday off, and I'm…just going to stay here and make my own turkey."

"Oh, you can't be alone on Thanksgiving."

Sure she could. People did it all the time.

"Mom...I want to be alone."

"Trina."

"I miss you," Trina said. "But I'm...my boyfriend just broke up with me and I need to be alone. Sort things through."

A beat passed. "Boyfriend?" Her mom sounded half amused, half horrified. "You were *dating* someone in Texas?"

"A cowboy even." Trina giggled, the sound morphing quickly into a choked sob. "I have to go."

"Call me again," her mom said quickly.

"I will, Mom." Trina hung up and collapsed back on her pillows, utterly spent. Too bad sleep wouldn't claim her, wouldn't alleviate this hollowness in her heart, this agony in her mind.

* * *

"I just need to know when Cal is scheduled to work here." Trina stood with her arms folded outside the U-shaped stable.

Brynn frowned at her but continued putting on her gloves. "His schedule isn't fixed like that."

Trina swallowed, the answer so unsatisfactory she couldn't even vocalize it.

"I know he won't be back until next week," she said.

"I might have to get a new job," Trina said. "I can't—" She cut off at Brynn's inquisitive look. "We broke up."

"Cal is a reasonable man—"

"I was the monarch butterfly and didn't tell him."

Brynn stalled in her twist back to stables, where she'd been going before Trina had caught her and asked to talk. "*You* were the butterfly? He must've talked to me about her a dozen times." A look close to exasperation crossed Brynn's face. "Maybe more."

Trina shuffled her feet. "Who else did he tell about the butterfly?"

"Everyone," Brynn said. "Squire and Kelly, Pete and Chelsea, even Bennett was speculating about who it could be."

"Hey, there, beautiful." Brynn's husband, Ethan, emerged from the stable and wrapped her in his arms. He placed a kiss on her temple, and every muscle in Trina's body constricted.

She pushed past them and went into the stable so they wouldn't see her cry.

"Is she okay?" she heard Ethan ask. Brynn responded, but Trina didn't hear it.

No, she thought. She is not okay.

But she worked through the pain, like she'd always done. She went to church by herself that next Sunday, knowing she wouldn't run into Cal. She managed to work another week out at the ranch without running into him. He had a bigger network of cowboys and spies, and she suspected he'd put them all on the case so their paths wouldn't cross.

She'd taken to eating her sandwiches in her car, windows rolled up, alone.

By the time she went home for Christmas, she was utterly spent. But she'd gone to church for several weeks, basked in that calming comfort, and she now knew how to pray for what she needed.

And for now, that would have to be enough.

Chapter Eleven

"How long do we have to keep doing this?" Bennett asked. "It's exhausting trying to keep tabs on a woman all day."

Cal didn't answer. Forever felt like too long, but also not long enough. He knew he was being petty. His brother had told him so. His mother too. In fact, everyone over the age of eighteen had told him to go talk to Trina and work things out.

On paper, it sounded like a good plan. But when he thought about actually coming face-to-face with her, his humiliation and hurt boiled up, making him angry. And he couldn't face her angry.

He also couldn't throw that blasted boot away. He'd tried, and it had lasted for half a day, whereupon he dug it out of the trashcan and put it back in its rightful spot.

"You stayin' here for the holidays?" Bennett asked, leaving the topic of Trina unanswered.

Cal picked up the clipboard outside a horse's stall. "Yep. You?"

"Yeah. My parents are going on a cruise for Christmas."

"Sounds fun." He checked the antibiotic dosage and went to get it ready. "I'll see you later."

"You should talk to her!" Bennett called after him. Cal didn't turn, or wave, or even slow his stride.

He just needed more time.

Petra had Sabrina for Christmas, and Cal would truly be alone. He hadn't given much thought to spending the holidays alone—not nearly as much as he usually did. He'd planned on holding hands with Trina, and sipping hot chocolate with Trina, and opening presents with Trina. He'd planned on it and didn't even know it. How was that even possible? How had he mapped out his whole future with her and not known?

He sighed as he leaned against a stall, his emotions overwhelming him and making him weak. "I just need more time," he muttered to himself. It had taken him four years to even start dating again. Truth was, Trina was the first woman who'd even sparked his attention. But he didn't know how to not be angry with her, and until he did, he didn't want to see her.

Christmas passed, and he enjoyed Heidi's cooking at

The Curse of February Fourteenth

the homestead. They laughed and played games and sang carols while Cal existed in the same space as them. He thought he did a decent job of putting on his *Happy Holidays!* face, but he caught the way Heidi watched him, saw Kelly and Chelsea with their heads bent together, and he escaped before the pies were even served.

Blitz and Bits didn't seem to mind that Trina wasn't around, and he let them up on the bed with him that night so he didn't have to sleep alone.

On New Year's Eve, he went over to Bennett and Sawyer's cabin for card games, chips and salsa, and a zero-tolerance policy for talk about women. Sawyer's girlfriend had broken up with him on the night of the masked ball, and he was still pretty salty about it.

Cal didn't think he'd stay until midnight. Number one, he was old and liked to get to bed by nine, because number two, he woke up at five-thirty no matter what time he actually went to sleep.

"Your turn," he said to Bennett for the third time since they'd started playing cards. He hastily set his phone down and played a card.

"Who are you texting?" Sawyer asked, making a swipe for Bennett's phone.

Bennett nearly hit it onto the floor in his attempt to get to it first. "No one."

"Better not be a woman."

Bennett shoved the phone in his back pocket and

hunkered down behind his cards. Which meant it totally was a woman.

Cal didn't ask any questions; didn't really care. He just wanted to be somewhere that felt like it had life, as his cabin had become immediately stale upon Trina's departure from his life.

Your choice, he told himself as he played a heart, the trump suit for this round. Sawyer growled in protest as Cal won the hand over his ace of diamonds. He stacked the cards in front of him, his mind still on Trina.

You could have her back.

He pushed his breath out in a slow stream. *Help me release my anger,* he prayed, something he'd been doing since Christmas. Every time he thought about the boot, he felt like the world's biggest loser. Every time he pictured Trina, all he could think about was how she'd lied to him. Over and over again.

And then he'd berate himself for not knowing. For not listening to his gut when it told him there was something she was hiding.

There was. A lot of somethings. Her inexperience for the job. That she was a world champion tennis player. Those things he could handle—he *had* handled.

But her being the butterfly and saying nothing....

He shook his head as he lost a round he should've won.

He left by ten and was sound asleep when the ball fell and the new year began.

The Curse of February Fourteenth

* * *

CAL STRONGLY DISLIKED January and half of February. Everyone had all these grand goals to work out, eat healthier, get organized. He kept his house sterile, and could eat whatever he wanted because he spent twelve hours a day on his feet. Check, check, and check.

Truth was, he hated January, because it meant February was coming, and that meant Valentine's Day. He thought five years would be enough to get over what Petra had done, but his heart felt twisted and poisoned inside his chest, and he wondered if his scars would ever heal completely.

At the dawn of February, Bennett approached him for their ten-thirty check-in. Cal had to work over at Brynn's today, and he did not want to run into Trina.

"This is the last day I'm doin' this, boss," Bennett said. "She's in the exercise yard, so I think you're good to go to the stables." His phone chimed, and he looked at it, a set of frown lines appearing between his eyes. "Did you know there's a Valentine's Day dance this year?"

Cal snorted. "How would I know that? And no, I'm not going."

Bennett barely looked up from his phone, and annoyance sang through Cal. He wanted to argue with Bennett that he needed him to keep tabs on Trina, but the fact was, he didn't. They'd perfected their come and go, ebb and flow routine, and he could avoid her easily now.

It had been a couple of weeks since he felt like he'd break apart if he saw her, so that was good. Time really did heal a lot of things.

His phone rang, and he plucked it from his pocket. Shock traveled through him in pulses when he saw Trina's name and face on the screen.

"You should answer that," Bennett said, peering at the phone's screen.

"And you should mind your own business." Cal sent the call to voicemail and left Bennett standing near the chicken coops.

Why would Trina call him? His phone bleeped out a sound, indicating that she'd left a message. In the next moment, his text sound rose into the sky.

Also Trina, and Cal's eyes caught the first part of her message.

Wanted to know if you would like

Cal resisted the urge to tap on the notification and read the whole thing. He made it all the way through the office building and into the stables before he lost his willpower and opened the message.

Wanted to know if you would like to go to the Valentine's Day dance with me. They're having it in the rec center.

Another dance? Was she serious? Did she want to make him the biggest laughingstock in Three Rivers?

Angrily, he shoved his phone in his back pocket and

The Curse of February Fourteenth

got to work. The faster he worked, the faster he finished. And the faster he finished, the sooner he could get on home, feed his dogs, and turn on a good documentary, one that would allow him a few minutes of relief from thinking about Trina.

Chapter Twelve

Trina had texted Bennett, Sawyer, and Brynn. Three times each. None of them could confirm that Cal was with them, and all of them said they'd tried talking to him about the Valentine's Day dance, and that he'd shut them down pretty quick.

Worry gnawed at her stomach. She really needed him to come to the dance. She'd volunteered to help put the event together, and she'd carefully guided the committee chairperson toward another dance, in the rec center, with a full dinner beforehand.

She looked at the pair of tickets hanging on the fridge. She'd bought them the day they'd gone on sale, and now the dinner-dance was sold out. Cal had never answered her text, and never returned her phone call.

She put a pot of water on the stove and got out a jar of spaghetti sauce and a box of noodles. When she'd gone home for Christmas, she'd told her family about Cal. About what she'd done and why. Her mother had suggested a way to make up with Cal, and Trina had gone down to the rec center to volunteer for the dance committee the day she'd arrived back in Three Rivers.

Now she just needed to get Cal there, with the boot he still kept on his mantel. So maybe she'd "strolled by" his cabin to check that he still had it. She couldn't describe the hope that had filled her chest when she found it still in its rightful place.

While the noodles cooked, she couldn't help walking over to the monarch butterfly wings hanging on the back of the closet door. They really were beautiful, and she really wanted to put them on and walk into the dance, her attention singular on Cal.

Which would be super hard to do if he wasn't there.

Helplessness filled her, and she turned away from the wings, away from her thoughts, as the water over-boiled and hissed against the hot burner. The smell of burnt starch filled the apartment, and Trina hurried to clean up the mess though her phone chimed three times in quick succession.

Anxiety urged her to wipe faster and twist the burner to a lower heat. Once that was done, she reached for her phone to find three messages from Bennett.

He won't come to the dance.

Maybe you should think of something else.

Sorry, Trina.

The Curse of February Fourteenth

The balloon of hope that had kept her going these past several weeks deflated all the way.

Sorry, Trina.

A freaky calmness descended over her, and she set the phone on the counter and resumed her preparation of the spaghetti. She stirred, drained noodles, and mixed everything together. She tonged herself a bowlful of food and sat down in front of her phone.

But her appetite had fled. The very smell of oregano set her stomach turning, and she pushed the bowl further from her.

All at once, an idea hit her.

If Cal wouldn't come to the dance, she'd go to him.

She scrambled to get her phone, where she sent a message to Bennett. *Do you want my tickets to the Valentine's Day dinner and dance?*

You're giving up?

You just told me he wouldn't come.

I didn't peg you for a quitter.

Oh, I'm not quitting. I'm just changing tactics. She'd done it many times during a match. If she couldn't wear her opponent out by hitting the ball from one corner to the other, she went for hard strokes right into the body. If that didn't work, she tried a short ball *barely* over the net. Or skipping the ball off the baseline. Challenging balls she knew were in. Complaining to the chair umpire. Whatever she had to do to get inside the head of the woman across the net.

Cal didn't have a tennis racquet, and Trina had tried appealing to a higher power to help her. So far, nothing had worked.

"But I'm not giving up," she said to the butterfly wings.

She marveled at this change in her. She'd fled her life when things went public with Carlos. Why was she willing to stay and fight for Cal when she hadn't before?

Because I love him.

The answer was as clear as glass, easy to understand, and like a balm to her weary soul. Tears pricked her eyes, and she decided to try one more prayer.

Please, she pleaded. Please help me to know what to do, and what to say, to get him to forgive me.

An idea popped into her mind, and she didn't hesitate. Simply grabbed the wings and marched out the front door.

Chapter Thirteen

Cal heard the knock on his cabin door, but he ignored it. He could feign sleep if Bennett poked his head in. Could pretend he hadn't heard the knock if it was anyone else.

Except this knocking got louder and louder. Whoever it was wasn't going away, so Cal heaved himself to his feet and crossed to the door.

He yanked it open and barked, "What?" onto the porch.

No one answered, but a glorious sight filled his eyes, making his heart thrum and his emotions spiral up and down, up and down.

Trina stood there, maskless, wearing that tight pair of black jeans and the matching tank top. She only wore one black boot with light blue stitching, and he instantly wanted to get the other one and slip it on her foot, dance the night away with her in his arms. The glittery, orange and black butterfly wings made her seem unearthly. A goddess.

He sucked in a breath. Just like that Halloween night, he felt a pull to her as strong as gravity. Though he tried to resist, he took one step toward her, unable to look away.

"I'm sorry," she said. "I was a different person the night of the masked ball, and I didn't want you to know that woman."

"I liked that woman," he said through a raw throat.

Trina flinched, almost like she hadn't expected him to speak. "I think you have my boot," she said. "I'd like it back." She moved as if she'd enter his cabin, but he stepped in front of her.

"You can't have the boot."

She met his eyes, challenge in hers. "Why not?"

"It's mine." Cal's nerves calmed, shooting only pulses of hot energy through him instead of vibrating like he'd been plugged in to a live wire. "This beautiful, mysterious woman left it behind, and I found it."

"You can't even wear it."

"I'm thinking of going around and having all the eligible ladies in town try it on, see if I can find out who it belongs to." He leaned in the doorway, a playful smile on his face.

Trina frowned more fully now. "I don't understand. You're not mad at me?"

"I'm furious with you," he said in a whisper. "But even angrier at myself."

"At yourself?"

"For holding onto that boot, daydreaming about some woman I didn't even know when I had a better one right in front of me."

She backed up a step, but Cal didn't want her to go. "Stay," he whispered. "Please stay."

"You're home alone?" She tried to see past him, but his frame filled the doorway, and she focused back on him.

"I'm always home alone," he said, agony in his tone. He was tired of being alone. Tired of fixing a sandwich for dinner. Tired of only having documentaries for companions.

"What about tomorrow night? Will you be alone then?" Trina asked, edging closer. "It's Valentine's Day."

He swallowed. "Not my finest day." In fact, he couldn't wait for it to be over. Then he wouldn't have to think about it again for a while.

"I think we should change that," she said, stepping fully toward him now. One, two. If she took a third, he'd be able to wrap his arms around her and hold her against his chest. Everything in him screamed at him to do that, but he remained as still as a statue.

She put her hand on his chest, effectively branding him. "Let's break this curse we both have on February fourteenth."

"How do you think we can do that?" He trailed one

finger along the edge of her wing. He'd wanted her to be the monarch butterfly so many times. The fact that she was should be comforting, not angering.

"See if that boot fits me." She peered up at him with those gorgeous eyes, and it took every ounce of self-control Cal had not to lean down and close the two inches between them and kiss her.

"I guess you can try it on," he said.

"If it fits, does that mean you're my Prince Charming?"

"I sure hope so," Cal said, backing into the cabin. He took the boot from the mantel and gestured for her to sit on the couch. She perched right on the edge of it and held up her shoeless foot. He knelt in front of her and slipped the boot on easily. He glanced up at her, the silence between them almost to the breaking point.

"I'm so sorry," she whispered at the same time he said, "I'm sorry, Trina."

She grinned, which caused Cal's chest to expand properly for the first time in months. "I'm going to kiss you now," she said only a moment before she touched her lips to his.

He took her face in his hands and matched the rhythm of her mouth, taking from her what he needed to be whole again. She seemed to be doing the same, and by the time she pulled away, Cal could finally breathe.

"I missed you," he said gruffly.

"Should've brought the boot over earlier, I suppose."

She giggled, and he swooped onto the couch next to her and held her tight against his chest.

"I felt like a fool," he said, going straight for the confession. "I was humiliated, and I—it took me a long time to come to terms with those feelings."

"Because of Petra." She wasn't asking.

"Because I wasn't sure how I'd fallen in love with you so fast."

She sucked in a breath and held it. "I'm a different person now."

"I know that."

"Do you still like that woman you met at the dance?"

"I sure do," Cal said, hoping he could explain. "She changed my world. She opened up my heart to the possibility of having another woman in my life. For years there, it was just me and Sabrina. No one else was invited. But she—*you*—changed that." He exhaled and stroked his fingers up and down her bare arm, a tiny thrill passing through him at the softness of her skin.

"So it was probably stupid, but I held onto the magic from that night. The butterfly was magic to me, and I didn't want to just discount her." He leaned over and brushed his lips along her temple, down to her ear.

"I wanted her to be you," he whispered. "Every day, I wanted her to be you."

She turned and looked him straight in the face. "I love you, Cal," she said. A nervous laugh burst from her mouth. "It sounds so strange, but I feel it." She tapped her chest, right above her heart. "The same way I felt so...peaceful at church the first time I went. Like it was just right."

Cal smiled, and the darkness that had been clouding inside his soul these past few months dissipated. "I know exactly what you mean." He ducked his head closer. "And now I'm going to kiss you."

This time, he explored her mouth gently, giving all of himself to the woman he loved.

Chapter Fourteen

"I looked you up online," Cal said after she'd arrived at his house with a couple of take-and-bake pizzas in the shape of hearts.

Trina seized, a guttural groan emanating from her throat. "It's Valentine's Day," she said, setting his oven to the correct temperature. "Do we have to talk about this today?"

He'd presented her with a dozen red roses at lunchtime and given her a German chocolate cupcake with a chocolate-dipped strawberry topper when she'd left the ranch after work. She just wanted to eat pizza and curl up with him on the couch. Maybe talk about the last documentary he'd watched or what the weather was like in London.

Anything but what he'd seen online.

"I just think you should know that I don't care who she

was," Cal said, clearly wanting to talk about everything Trina didn't.

She turned to face him and crossed her arms. "You aren't impressed with her serve? Her multiple Grand Slam wins? Her millions of dollars?"

He didn't even blink. "Nope."

"What do you like about her?"

"That she came here." He gave her a sexy smile and extended his hand toward her, an invitation to go with him. And because Trina loved him and wanted to be near him, she slipped her fingers in between his and let him lead her out to the front porch.

He sighed as he sat on the top step, drawing her down with him. "I don't care about the serve, or the titles, or the money."

"I know you don't." She leaned her head against his shoulder, glad for an easy place to land when things got hard.

"I do want to see the trophy room in your house in California."

She tensed. He'd done more than look her up online. He'd read articles. "It's boring," she said. "All this gold and silver the light glints off of. Bad for the eyes."

"What are you going to do about that house?" he asked.

"I don't know. Sell it, I guess."

"Because you're staying here, right?"

The Curse of February Fourteenth

She looked over to him at the nervous undertone in his words. "Cal, of course I'm staying here."

"I live in a two-bedroom cabin," he said. "It's not a house in the hills. Not even close."

She lifted her chin and glanced down the gravel path toward the homestead. "Hills are overrated."

He chuckled and lifted her knuckles to his lips. "I'm so glad you came to Three Rivers," he murmured, moving his mouth to her wrist.

"Me too," she said.

"I may not be glad about how we got here, but the important thing is that we did. We survived." He looked at her, and she caught a desperate edge in his eye.

"We sure did," she said.

"So money or no money, titles or no titles, fame or no fame, I'm glad you're here." He gave her a small smile and dropped his gaze to the steps in front of him.

She stood, an idea blooming in her head. "Come on," she said, tugging on his hand to get him to come with her.

"What?" he asked as she towed him back into the house.

She glanced around, but could only find the television as a source of music. "You don't have a radio?" she asked.

"A radio? No, I don't have a radio."

"We'll use my phone."

"For what?" he asked as she hurried over to where she'd left it on the kitchen table. She swiped and tapped, typed in a website, and made sure the volume was turned up all the way.

The first notes of the ballad came through the speakers, and Cal's gaze turned hot. "I'm wearing the boots," she said with a smile. "I want to dance."

He took her easily into his arms, and she melted into his embrace. She'd spoken true when she'd said being with him just felt right. They swayed to the music they'd first danced to at the masked ball, the magic between them just as powerful now as it had been then. And despite some bumps and bruises along the way, Trina truly felt like a princess who had gotten her prince.

Keep reading for a sneak peek of the next book in the Three Rivers Ranch Romance™ series, **Fifteen Minutes of Fame**.

Sneak Peek! Fifteen Minutes of Fame Chapter One

Navy Richards drew in a deep breath as the ticket attendant made his way toward her. He seemed nice, fatherly, probably bored to death. He punched tickets and made small talk, but Navy didn't feel any of the man's calm energy. She gripped her ticket to Three Rivers, Texas for all she was worth, wondering for the hundredth time if she'd decided correctly.

Yes, she thought, reassuring herself for the hundred and first time. She needed a break from her insane job as a pediatric nurse. Needed a break from the dozens of dating apps she had uninstalled just the previous night. Needed a break from her perfect younger sister, her gorgeous husband, and their new baby—which Navy had helped deliver and then care for while her sister sat in the hospital bed like a celebrity.

Familiar jealousy, bitterness, and frustration rose

through her throat, and Navy didn't like it. She didn't want to feel that way about her only sister. About anyone. She'd prayed more often than she'd doubted her decision to take the leave of absence and move hundreds of miles away for six months.

Her feelings would subside for a few days, and then they came back—seemingly stronger and louder than before.

"Ticket?"

Navy pulled herself from her thoughts and extended her ticket toward the attendant. She had to force her fingers to loosen so he could take it and punch it. He didn't linger with her, didn't ask her why she was going to Three Rivers—a small speck of a city—on a bus, didn't ask her how long she was staying. A sting started behind her heart, and Navy sighed as she leaned her head against the window and watched the Texas wilderness roll by.

She couldn't help her fantasies of finding and marrying a good man. She'd been working hard at it, going out with everyone who asked, signing up for every available dating app, kept as many evenings free as possible. At this point, she'd probably been out with every available bachelor in Austin.

"Time for a change," she whispered to her faint reflection in the glass. And so what if the change she wanted included a matchmaker? Why did Lexie get to dictate to Navy how she found her perfect catch? But her younger sister had definitely had plenty to say about Navy's decision to travel to Three Rivers and meet with an eighty-three-year-old matchmaker. None of it was nice. Or supportive. Or what Navy wanted to hear.

After all, not everyone could get married, live in a quaint brick home with a white picket fence, and have a baby whenever they wanted by age twenty-eight. Oh, no. Navy was several years older than that and had practically handed Lexie her husband on a silver platter.

She eradicated the thought of Scott before it could sour her mood further. She drew in another breath, prepared for anything once she arrived in Three Rivers.

Eight hours and two very stiff legs later, Navy disembarked from the bus in Three Rivers, Texas. The night air tasted wonderful. She turned in a circle, drinking in the bright lights of the bus station and the way she felt so *free* here.

Navy beamed at the park across the street, but it darkness didn't offer her a particularly nice welcome. Maybe coming here to meet with a matchmaker *was* a dumb idea. But it could also incite the change Navy needed in her life. Legend or not. Myth or not. Fantasy or fact. Navy didn't care. She believed in the magic of this place, and she wasn't going to let Lexie's poisoned lectures influence her.

The bus rumbled away, leaving Navy alone on the sidewalk, all of her bags with her. Reality descended, and she put on her backpack, shouldered her purse and then another bag, and tilted the wheeled suitcase behind her. The fact that she could fit her whole life into a few bags had surprised and saddened her, but now she felt liberated. She crossed the street without looking for traffic, because it seemed the downtown area where she'd arrived had already closed for the evening.

As she arrived at the fountain, she did notice one establishment with bright lights still on. The restaurant also boasted loud country music when the front doors opened and a couple spilled onto the street. They didn't glance in her direction, and in the next moment, the lights dimmed and left Navy to herself.

The stories about how women came here to find their true love had given Navy more hope than she'd had in five years. And that couple? Maybe it was a sign that she'd find her happily-ever-after in this place she'd never dreamed of visiting.

Her own aunt had convinced her that the trip to Three Rivers was warranted. She'd found her husband after a meeting with the very person Navy had an appointment with the following day. She looked around the park, imagining the tea lights her aunt had detailed, the summer dances that brought out all the cowboys from the nearby ranches.

Navy sighed, thinking maybe she'd meet the just-right man for her too, somewhere in Austin in a park like this, after her meeting tomorrow morning.

A smile stole across Navy's face, and she unburdened herself from her baggage. She cast a quick glance around to see if anyone was watching. She didn't think nine-thirty

The Curse of February Fourteenth

was late, but apparently for this small town, and it being a weeknight, it was.

She twirled and danced her way down the sidewalk, a low hum in the back of her throat. A sense of wonderment and magic infected her, and she just knew tonight was the first night of the rest of her life. That she'd just finally done something to find the right person.

A gasp of desperation ended her dance and she stilled next to her suitcases. She didn't want millions of dollars. She didn't need a big mansion. She spent fifty hours a week cradling and caring for babies, and she wanted one of her own. She wanted a husband to gaze at her with so much love, the way the new dads did in labor and delivery. They could live in a basement for all she cared.

Please let this work, she said to the stars before bending and collecting her belongings. She'd told the people she was renting a cottage from she'd be there by ten, and she had a few blocks to walk before arriving.

Thank you, she thought through every step. *Thank you for giving me this opportunity in Three Rivers, Texas.*

* * *

THE FOLLOWING MORNING further proved to Navy that she'd moved into a shack. Last night, the darkness had obscured the grime, the fact that the linoleum cracked in front of the stove and peeled where it met the carpet.

She'd rented the "cottage" from natives of Three

Rivers for further luck in her quest to find a husband. The Shepherd's had met her on the front porch and helped her carry her bags out to the cottage, which sat in a corner of their large, impressive yard. A rutted dirt lane led back to the cottage, and Navy needed to find some mode of transportation besides her feet.

Or maybe she wouldn't. She had her laptop, and the cottage did have electricity and Internet, so she was pretty set. She wasn't planning to work while in town, as she'd only be here for six months. Really, she needed an escape from her life, a vacation to reset herself. So that when she returned to Austin she'd be ready to be the kind of woman a man couldn't resist.

She left the cottage and it's lukewarm showers in favor of the late March Texas sunshine. Nothing could ruin today. Because today, Navy was meeting with Nancy Redd, the matchmaker who had promised Aunt Izzie that she'd marry a cowboy and live on a ranch. Navy wasn't sure if ranch life was what she wanted, necessarily, but she believed Nancy could give her a push in the right direction.

Aunt Izzie and Uncle Marvin had lived here in Three Rivers for about a decade after their wedding. Then they'd moved to Dripping Springs, a small town about an hour west of Austin, to be closer to family. Uncle Marvin had worked at Three Rivers Ranch, which Navy's cousin Heidi owned.

As she approached the address she'd been given,

The Curse of February Fourteenth

Navy's heart pounded with anticipation. Her footsteps slowed as she contemplated what Nancy would tell her. Her throat turned dry at the horrifying thought that perhaps there wasn't a match for her on this earth.

The house came into view, and it was obviously well kept. Clipped, green grass went right up to the street, where a mailbox stood straight and strong. A two-story house in pale blue boasted a bright red star above the front window. Rose bushes lined the sidewalk to the porch and along the front of the house. The only thing that seemed out of place was a birdhouse that looked like it had been put together by a bottle of Elmer's glue, a vat of popsicle sticks, and gallons of finger paint.

She gave the ugly lawn decoration a wary glance. Something drew her toward it and she stepped across the grass to examine it further. It sat up between a rose bush bearing peachy-colored blossoms and one with pink the color of lemonade. She couldn't quite reach the birdhouse, but she didn't really want to touch it.

"You like that birdhouse?"

Navy spun toward the masculine voice and took in the form of a man several inches taller than her and wide enough to block the sun. He wore a cowboy hat the color of graphite and a dark beard salted with loads of gray. Instant attraction sprang through her system at his maturity, at the scent of his cologne as it stuck in the air surrounding them.

He watched her with a pair of dark, dangerous eyes, clearly waiting for something.

She jolted to attention as embarrassment rushed to her face, heating it to the color of the red roses at the end of the line. "Oh, the birdhouse." She looked at the hideous thing again. "It's...did their grandson make it?"

He tilted his head to the side, confusion evident in his expression. "What do you mean?"

"It's crafty."

"Crafty?"

Navy got the impression that she'd said all the wrong things. "It looks...unique."

He crossed his arms, which only served to make his muscles that much more impressive. "It *is* unique. One of a kind, in fact."

"That's a relief." Navy added a short burst of laughter to her statement in an attempt to smooth things over with this man. "Well, I have an appointment, so I should get going." She hooked her thumb over her shoulder and backed away from the man for a few steps before turning around completely.

She felt the weight of his stare on her back, but she hadn't come here to impress a surly cowboy with strange questions about a clearly dysfunctional birdhouse.

No, she'd come here to find her soul mate, and there was only one person who could help her do that. So with a determined breath, she rounded the house and entered the door on the side, just as instructed.

The Curse of February Fourteenth

* * *

A carpenter cowboy who hates the history of his town, the nurse who comes because of the history, and the runaway horse that brings them together in unexpected ways...

Look for FIFTEEN MINUTES OF FAME by scanning the QR code below!

Second Chance Ranch: A Three Rivers Ranch Romance™ (Book 1): After his deployment, injured and discharged Major Squire Ackerman returns to Three Rivers Ranch, wanting to forgive Kelly for ignoring him a decade ago. He'd like to provide the stable life she needs, but with old wounds opening and a ranch on the brink of financial collapse, it will take patience and faith to make their second chance possible.

Third Time's the Charm: A Three Rivers Ranch Romance™ (Book 2): First Lieutenant Peter Marshall has a truckload of debt and no way to provide for a family, but Chelsea helps him see past all the obstacles, all the scars. With so many unknowns, can Pete and Chelsea develop the love, acceptance, and faith needed to find their happily ever after?

Fourth and Long: A Three Rivers Ranch Romance™ (Book 3): Commander Brett Murphy goes to Three Rivers Ranch to find some rest and relaxation with his Army buddies. Having his ex-wife show up with a seven-year-old she claims is his son is anything but the R&R he craves. Kate needs to make amends, and Brett needs to find forgiveness, but are they too late to find their happily ever after?

Fifth Generation Cowboy: A Three Rivers Ranch Romance™ (Book 4): Tom Lovell has watched his friends find their true happiness on Three Rivers Ranch, but everywhere he looks, he only sees friends. Rose Reyes has been bringing her daughter out to the ranch for equine therapy for months, but it doesn't seem to be working. Her challenges with Mari are just as frustrating as ever. Could Tom be exactly what Rose needs? Can he remove his friendship blinders and find love with someone who's been right in front of him all this time?

Sixth Street Love Affair: A Three Rivers Ranch Romance™ (Book 5): After losing his wife a few years back, Garth Ahlstrom thinks he's ready for a second chance at love. But Juliette Thompson has a secret that could destroy their budding relationship. Can they find the strength, patience, and faith to make things work?

The Seventh Sergeant: A Three Rivers Ranch Romance™ (Book 6): Life has finally started to settle down for Sergeant Reese Sanders after his devastating injury overseas. Discharged from the Army and now with a good job at Courage Reins, he's finally found happiness—until a horrific fall puts him right back where he was years ago: Injured and depressed. Carly Watters, Reese's new veteran care coordinator, dislikes small towns almost as much as she loathes cowboys. But she finds herself faced with both when she gets assigned to Reese's case. Do they have the humility and faith to make their relationship more than professional?

Eight Second Ride: A Three Rivers Ranch Romance™ (Book 7): Ethan Greene loves his work at Three Rivers Ranch, but he can't seem to find the right woman to settle down with. When sassy yet vulnerable Brynn Bowman shows up at the ranch to recruit him back to the rodeo circuit, he takes a different approach with the barrel racing champion. His patience and newfound faith pay off when a friendship--and more--starts with Brynn. But she wants out of the rodeo circuit right when Ethan wants to rejoin. Can they find the path God wants them to take and still stay together?

The Ninth Inning: A Three Rivers Ranch Romance™ (Book 8): The Christmas season has never felt like such a burden to boutique owner Andrea Larsen. But with Mama gone and the holidays upon her, Andy finds herself wishing she hadn't been so quick to judge her former boyfriend, cowboy Lawrence Collins. Well, Lawrence hasn't forgotten about Andy either, and he devises a plan to get her out to the ranch so they can reconnect. Do they have the faith and humility to patch things up and start a new relationship?

Ten Days in Town: A Three Rivers Ranch Romance™ (Book 9): Sandy Keller is tired of the dating scene in Three Rivers. Though she owns the pancake house, she's looking for a fresh start, which means an escape from the town where she grew up. When her older brother's best friend, Tad Jorgensen, comes to town for the holidays, it is a balm to his weary soul. A helicopter tour guide who experienced a near-death experience, he's looking to start over too--but in Three Rivers. Can Sandy and Tad navigate their troubles to find the path God wants them to take--and discover true love--in only ten days?

Eleven Year Reunion: A Three Rivers Ranch Romance™ (Book 10): Pastry chef extraordinaire, Grace Lewis has moved to Three Rivers to help Heidi Ackerman open a bakery in Three Rivers. Grace relishes the idea of starting over in a town where no one knows about her failed cupcakery. She doesn't expect to run into her old high school boyfriend, Jonathan Carver. A carpenter working at Three Rivers Ranch, Jon's in town against his will. But with Grace now on the scene, Jon's thinking life in Three Rivers is suddenly looking up. But with her focus on baking and his disdain for small towns, can they make their eleven year reunion stick?

The Twelfth Town: A Three Rivers Ranch Romance™ (Book 11): Newscaster Taryn Tucker has had enough of life on-screen. She's bounced from town to town before arriving in Three Rivers, completely alone and completely anonymous--just the way she now likes it. She takes a job cleaning at Three Rivers Ranch, hoping for a chance to figure out who she is and where God wants her. When she meets happy-go-lucky cowhand Kenny Stockton, she doesn't expect sparks to fly. Kenny's always been "the best friend" for his female friends, but the pull between him and Taryn can't be denied. Will they have the courage and faith necessary to make their opposite worlds mesh?

Lucky Number Thirteen: A Three Rivers Ranch Romance™ (Book 12): Tanner Wolf, a rodeo champion ten times over, is excited to be riding in Three Rivers for the first time since he left his philandering ways and found religion. Seeing his old friends Ethan and Brynn is therapuetic--until a terrible accident lands him in the hospital. With his rodeo career over, Tanner thinks maybe he'll stay in town--and it's not just because his nurse, Summer Hamblin, is the prettiest woman he's ever met. But Summer's the queen of first dates, and as she looks for a way to make a relationship with the transient rodeo star work Summer's not sure she has the fortitude to go on a second date. Can they find love among the tragedy?

The Curse of February Fourteenth: A Three Rivers Ranch Romance™ (Book 13): Cal Hodgkins, cowboy veterinarian at Bowman's Breeds, isn't planning to meet anyone at the masked dance in small-town Three Rivers. He just wants to get his bachelor friends off his back and sit on the sidelines to drink his punch. But when he sees a woman dressed in gorgeous butterfly wings and cowgirl boots with blue stitching, he's smitten. Too bad she runs away from the dance before he can get her name, leaving only her boot behind...

Fifteen Minutes of Fame: A Three Rivers Ranch Romance™ (Book 14): Navy Richards is thirty-five years of tired—tired of dating the same men, working a demanding job, and getting her heart broken over and over again. Her aunt has always spoken highly of the matchmaker in Three Rivers, Texas, so she takes a six-month sabbatical from her high-stress job as a pediatric nurse, hops on a bus, and meets with the matchmaker. Then she meets Gavin Redd. He's handsome, he's hardworking, and he's a cowboy. But is he an Aquarius too? Navy's not making a move until she knows for sure...

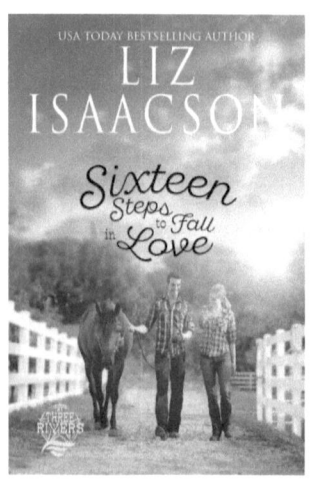

Sixteen Steps to Fall in Love: A Three Rivers Ranch Romance™ (Book 15): A chance encounter at a dog park sheds new light on the tall, talented Boone that Nicole can't ignore. As they get to know each other better and start to dig into each other's past, Nicole is the one who wants to run. This time from her growing admiration and attachment to Boone. From her aging parents. From herself.

But Boone feels the attraction between them too, and he decides he's tired of running and ready to make Three Rivers his permanent home. **Can Boone and Nicole use their faith to overcome their differences and find a happily-ever-after together?**

The Sleigh on Seventeenth Street: A Three Rivers Ranch Romance™ (Book 16): A cowboy with skills as an electrician tries a relationship with a down-on-her luck plumber. Can Dylan and Camila make water and electricity play nicely together this Christmas season? Or will they get shocked as they try to make their relationship work?

The First Lady of Three Rivers Ranch: A Three Rivers Ranch Romance™ (Book 17): Heidi Duffin has been dreaming about opening her own bakery since she was thirteen years old. She scrimped and saved for years to afford baking and pastry school in San Francisco. And now she only has one year left before she's a certified pastry chef. Frank Ackerman's father has recently retired, and he's taken over the largest cattle ranch in the Texas Panhandle. A horseman through and through, he's also nearing thirty-one and looking for someone to bring love and joy to a homestead that's been dominated by men for a decade. But when he convinces Heidi to come clean the cowboy cabins, she changes all that. But the siren's call of a bakery is still loud in Heidi's ears, even if she's also seeing a future with Frank. Can she rely on her faith in ways she's never had to before or will their relationship end when summer does?

Second Generation in Three Rivers Romance™ Series

Step back into the heartwarming small Texas town of Three Rivers! This beloved town has captured the hearts of 2.5 million readers and caught the eye of Sony Pictures, and now a new generation of cowboys and cowgirls is ready to take center stage. Scan the QR code below with your phone to check out this new series!

1. The Cowboy Who Came Home - featuring Squire's son, Finn from SECOND CHANCE RANCH!

Seven Sons Ranch in Three Rivers Romance™ Series

Meet the cowboy billionaire brothers at Seven Sons Ranch! Scan the QR code below with your phone to check out this complete series.

1. Rhett
2. Tripp
3. Liam
4. Jeremiah
5. Wyatt
6. Skyler
7. Micah
8. Gideon

Shiloh Ridge Ranch in Three Rivers Romance™ Series

Meet the cowboy billionaires in the southern hills outside of Three Rivers! Scan the QR code below with your phone to check out this complete series.

1. The Mechanics of Mistletoe
2. The Horsepower of the Holiday
3. The Construction of Cheer
4. The Secret of Santa
5. The Gift of Gingerbread
6. The Harmony of Holly
7. The Chemistry of Christmas
8. The Delivery of Decor
9. The Blessing of Babies
10. The Networking of the Nativity
11. The Wrangling of the Wreath
12. The Hope of Her Heart

About Liz

Liz Isaacson writes inspirational romance, usually set in Texas, or Wyoming, or anywhere else horses and cowboys exist. She lives in Utah, where she writes full-time, takes her two dogs to the park everyday, and eats a lot of veggies while writing. Find her on her website at feelgoodfiction-books.com

www.ingramcontent.com/pod-product-compliance
Lightning Source LLC
LaVergne TN
LVHW041637060526
838200LV00040B/1609